Oh, Those Bradys!

There's bedlam in the TV studio. Carol and Mike Brady have just said yes, they *will* come back for next week's round of "Stunts & Stumpers." The band breaks in, the audience breaks out—with cheers and screams. Carol throws a kiss. Mike feels like throwing his lunch.

But what's this ruckus in front of the set at home? Marcia, Jan, and Cindy say their *mom* is the greatest. Greg, Peter, and Bobby say their *dad* is the greatest.

And "Oh!" moans Alice, the Brady maid. "Don't you see what's happened, you poor tykes? Your parents are in show biz. Go to bed and cover your heads!"

THE BRADY BUNCH

Watch the hit show on ABC-TV with the following cast:

MIKE BRADY . . . . . ROBERT REED
CAROL BRADY . . . . FLORENCE HENDERSON
ALICE . . . . ANN B. DAVIS
GREG BRADY . . . . BARRY WILLIAMS
PETER BRADY . . . . CHRIS KNIGHT
BOBBY BRADY . . . MIKE LOOKINLAND
JAN BRADY . . . . . EVE PLUMB
CINDY BRADY . . . . SUSAN OLSEN
MARCIA BRADY . . . MAUREEN McCORMICK

Executive Producer—Sherwood Schwartz
In Color

A Paramount Production In association with Redwood Productions, Inc.

The Brady Bunch

William Johnston

LANCER BOOKS NEW YORK

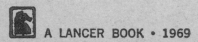 A LANCER BOOK • 1969

THE BRADY BUNCH

LANCER BOOKS, INC. • 1560 BROADWAY
NEW YORK, N.Y. 10036

1.

In general, there was nothing particularly unusual about the Brady family. They lived in paradise, also known officially as California. And in a castle, more prosaically referred to by most designers and builders as a ranch house. And, counting all, there were eleven of them: two senior adults, six minor children, one combination maid, babysitter and handywoman, one irrespressible dog, and one eccentric cat. So, in general, a family couldn't get much more ordinary.

The hitch was that the boys in the Brady family were related to the girls in the Brady family only by marriage—and the same for the dog and cat. Which was not to say that the boys and girls and dog and cat were married to each other. The boys and girls, ranging in age from thirteen to five, were, of course, too young to be married to anybody. And the dog and cat were of the opinion that although marriage was probably perfectly fine for humans, it was impractical for animals, who seldom seemed to be able to get up the two dollars for a marriage license. The explanation was that when the senior male, Mike Brady, married the senior female, now Carol Brady, he was already the father of three boys, and she was already the mother of three girls. According to the Bureau of Statistics, the odds against such a seemingly disastrous mixing-together happening were something like twenty-seven zillion-to-one. But then, as some guest at the wedding undoubtedly said, marriages are made in heaven, not at the Bureau of Statistics.

In spite of all the obvious potential for problems, the marriage and the mixture were working out fairly well. Not that incidents hadn't occurred. For example, the dog and the cat had pretty much destroyed the dignity of the marriage ceremony by getting involved in a brouhaha that had resulted in frightening most of the guests half to death and dumping the wedding cake in the groom's face. And Mike and Carol on their wedding night had discovered that they were so lonesome for the family that they had gone and got it, so that the honeymoon suite of the hotel that night was occupied not only by the happy couple but also by the boys, Greg, Peter and Bobby, and the girls, Marcia, Jan and Cindy, and the maid, Alice, and the dog, Tiger, and the cat, Fluffy.

Such incidents were history now, however. And all of the members of the bunch were confident that they had learned from them, to the extent that they were fairly sure that they would not repeat them, in any form. In fact, so mellowed were they by experience that now, facing the third week of living together, they had no doubts whatsoever about the future. In other words, they were cocky—and asking for it!

In the master bedroom, Mike Brady stood in front of the dresser mirror, dressing to go out. He was tying his tie for the fourth time. The first three times, the small end had come out considerably longer than the large end. Mike was a tall, trimly built man, with dark hair and an agreeable face. He was approaching middle age, which is to say 38, getting close enough to reach it without having to strain. When he was not wholly involved in being the father of the family, he occupied himself as an architect. A study of his expression at the moment left the impression that perhaps his inability to tie the tie correctly had roots in something more than ineptness. It would not have been unreasonable to suspect that he was not looking forward to going out, and that, consciously or subconsciously, he was delaying the moment of departure as long as possible.

Carol Brady came bustling into the room. Carol was the same age, approximately, as Mike. But it was obvious that, by sheer grit, she would remain on the bright side of middle age much longer. Carol was attractive in most aspects, but it was her smile that made her most noticeable, and most appealing. It always seemed spontaneous, and could best be described as a flower bursting into bloom. Noting the trouble her husband was having with his tie, Carol halted on her way to the closet and observed his efforts to get

7

the two ends to come out close to even at the bottom.

"If you don't want to go to this show, why don't you just say so?" Carol asked, amused.

Mike looked back over his shoulder at her. "What brought on that comment?" he asked.

"You've never had that much difficulty tying your tie before," she replied, moving on toward the closet. "When I left here ten minutes ago, you were right where you are right now. You're procrastinating."

Mike laughed lightly, then faced the mirror again. "As a matter of fact," he said, attacking the tie-tying project once more, "I *did* tell you I don't want to go to this show. When I got home this evening, you said, 'Mike, I got two free tickets to "Stunts & Stumpers," do you want to go?' and I said, 'No.' I don't see how I could be any more specific than that."

Carol had opened the closet door and got down an evening bag from the shelf. "But I've never been to a TV show—not 'live,'" she responded.

"Oh? How dead were you the last time?"

"You know what I mean. It'll be fun. I've seen the show a couple times on TV, and it's a ball. Really. Everybody seems to be having such a good time. The m.c. and the contestants and the audience . . . everybody. Besides, it wouldn't be fair to Maggie if we didn't go."

Mike was looking disgustedly at his tie in the mirror. Distracted, listening to Carol, he had managed to tie it correctly. "Oh, well . . ." He shrugged. He walked to where his wife was standing,

8

at the open closet door, rummaging in her evening purse, and kissed her affectionately on the forehead. "Maggie?" he asked. "What does your girlfriend have to do with it?"

"Frank is out of town on a business trip," Carol replied, still going through the bag.

Mike reached past her, into the closet for his jacket, then paused in midreach. "Now, wait a minute—we have to go to 'Stunts & Stumpers,' because it wouldn't be fair to Maggie if we didn't because her husband is out of town on a business trip? You must be leaving *something* out."

"That's where I got the tickets—from Maggie," Carol explained. "Where did you think?"

"Frankly, I didn't give it much thought," Mike answered, finally getting the jacket from the closet. "If I had, though, I probably would have guessed that the show hired a muscleman to go from door to door forcing free tickets on innocent and defenseless citizens. The only way anybody would get me to take a ticket to 'Stunts'—"

"Have you seen my going-out key," Carol asked, breaking in.

"Your what?"

"The door key I take when we go out in the evening. I have a key I take when I go out during the day and a key I take when we go out during the evening. You don't wear the same shoes when we go out in the evening that you wear when you go to work, do you?"

Mike shook his head. "I haven't seen it. Is it patent leather?"

Carol laughed. "It isn't any dressier than the

other key," she said. "Are you about ready?"

"About," Mike nodded, going to the dresser to get his wallet. "May I have one more question? Why would it be such a tragedy for Maggie if we didn't see the show?"

"Well, she went to all the trouble of getting the tickets. She adores 'Stunts & Stumpers.' It's her all-time favorite quiz show, and Jackie Jackson is her all-time favorite m.c. And then, early this afternoon, Frank called and told her he had to go to Chicago on business—right away. Well, of course, Maggie was heartbroken. I've never seen her so really devastated. She—"

"Just the facts, ma'am," Mike begged.

"Oh. Okay. So, to make a long story short, I'm her best friend, she says, so she gave the tickets to me. Understand?"

"Well . . . I understand why Frank left town," Mike replied, smiling. "I wish somebody had warned me—I could be on a plane to Chicago right now." He opened the bedroom door, then stepped back to allow his wife to precede him.

"I'm glad I know you're not serious," Carol said, breezing past him.

"But I am, I am."

"Mike, if you knew yourself as well as I know you," Carol said, leading the way along the hallway, "you'd know that you're not. What you're really doing when you say all those unpleasant things about quiz shows is treating me to a display of your incisive wit."

Mike dropped the argument. To have continued it would have been to expose himself to the danger of revealing to his wife that perhaps his wit was not really so incisive.

At the moment that Mike and Carol were leaving the master bedroom, the other members of the Brady bunch were occupying what in various households was called the playroom or recreation room. They were more or less grouped around a television set that was tuned to the channel that later would broadcast "Stunts & Stumpers." The object was to take no chance whatsoever on missing the program. There was general belief in the group that if they kept their attention fixed to the screen they would be able to catch a glimpse of Mike and Carol in the audience—at least for one six-millionth of a second.

Alice, the maid, was seated in the center of the couch that faced the set. She was watching, with absolutely no interest at all, the program on the screen—a twelfth rerun of "Superman." Alice had already achieved middle age. Consequently, a lot of her had settled to the bottom. She showed no evidence of having become bitter about that fact, however. Her face, now, as most of the time, was decorated with a look of overall contentment and a smile as big as all outdoors.

To Alice's right, seated as close to her as possible, was Cindy, the youngest girl. Like her two sisters, Cindy was blonde. With good reason, Cindy looked as if she might lisp at the drop of an 's.' On the other side of Alice, dark-haired and momentarily intense (and for good reason: Clark Kent had just disappeared into a corridor closet), was

11

the youngest boy in the bunch, Bobby. He was not seated quite as close to Alice as Cindy was, but the program had not been in progress long, and as soon as the action heated up it was a good bet that he would begin sliding nearer.

The two older children, Greg and Marcia, were having nothing to do with what was happening on the television screen. They were much too mature these days to have any truck with Superman. As a matter of fact, Greg had reached such a state of advanced maturity that he had recently chalked on the recreation room blackboard the needling comment: Superman Wears Long Underwear! And Marcia was so far above such juvenile fare that she had even considered Greg's attempt to belittle Superman to be somewhat childish. They were seated on the floor in a spot where they could not see the screen (if they had been able to see it, they might have been tempted to sneak looks), engaged in a fierce battle of Scrabble. And, talk about maturity, Greg had just built the word *gland*.

The other two youngsters, the middle children, Jan and Peter, were in different parts of the room, involved in different pasttimes. Jan was transferring the yellow ribbon that had been put around Fluffy's neck in the morning from Fluffy's tail, where it had been tied by Peter along toward afternoon, back to Fluffy's neck. And Peter, gently massaging Tiger's back-of-the-neck and staring into space, was working exceedingly hard at looking relaxed, innocent and totally oblivious.

That was the scene as Mike and Carol entered

the playroom. Their appearance completely destroyed it, however. The two middle children and the two youngest children immediately jumped up and ran to them. And Tiger, never one to miss any festivity no matter how little it concerned him, bounded after Peter and galloped across the Scrabble board, scattering letters in all directions.

"Alith thays we can thtay up, Mommy!" Cindy announced.

"Oh? Why? Isn't that a little late?" Carol replied, directing the question to Alice.

"When are they ever going to get another chance to see you on TV?" Alice replied. "I considered the possibility that some big Hollywood producer would see you in the audience and star you in his next extravaganza, and then, next year, the children could see it when it turns up on the 'Late Late Show.' But then I said to myself, 'Naaaaaah, it'll never happen,' and I decided to let them stay up late and see you tonight."

"I think your reasoning is excellent," Carol nodded. "So be it."

"Mom, try to get on the program," Jan said. "They have some real groovy prizes. Betty Baker, a friend of mine's mother, was on one of those shows and she won a whole year's supply of pipe cleaners."

Carol peered at her questioningly. "The kind of pipes that men smoke or the kind of pipes that water runs through?"

Jan frowned. "Gee, Betty didn't say."

"Well, either kind," Mike said, "that's the sort

of prize I'd give a year's growth to win—now that I've stopped growing."

"That's very witty," Marcia told him. She was on her knees, picking up Scrabble pieces. "You say a lot of very incisive things, you know, Mike."

"I'm often told that," he answered, smiling blandly. "But, even though a whole year's supply of pipe cleaners is the kind of prize that's worth getting in there and fighting for, don't expect us to appear on the program. In the first place, those contestants are picked a long time beforehand. And, in the second place—"

"They say they pick them from the audience, Dad," Greg said, addressing his father from under a coffee table, where he had gone to retrieve several Scrabble letters.

"Son, I think you're old enough to know about euphemisms," Mike told him. "A euphemism is something people say when they don't care to say what they really mean. For instance, when an ordinary person does something very strange, we usually say he's a nut. But if a very rich person does something very strange, we more often than not say he's—a what? What's the word?"

"We say he's a euphemism," Peter said.

"No. No, no, you're not quite getting the hang of it. We say he's an eccentric. That's a euphemism."

"An eccentric is a euphemism?" Marcia said doubtfully.

"Forget it," Carol said to her. "I'll explain it to you tomorrow." She moved toward the exit. "Behave, everybody—we'll see you later."

14

"I always thought a euphemism was somebody who belonged to an Arab religion," Alice mused.

Mike, about to join Carol on the way out, halted. "How could you ever get anything like— oh, I know what you're thinking about. The Euphrates. That's a river somewhere. But I don't think—"

"Mike, come on," Carol urged.

"Dad," Greg called, "what were you going to tell me about euphemisms?" He was emerging from under the coffee table, both hands clutching Scrabble pieces.

"All I was going to say was," Mike replied, stopping again, "that when a TV show says its contestants are selected from the audience, that's sort of a euphemism. They might mean anything. The contestants could be the producer's brothers-in-law and sisters-in-law or the second cameraman's ex-wives."

"Oh, Mike, don't tell him that—that's not true," Carol protested.

"Well, one thing is obvious," Mike said. "Those contestants certainly aren't picked at random from the audience. If you've seen more than one quiz show, it's obvious that those people are picked because they all have one outstanding trait—they're all exhibitionists."

"What'th that?" Cindy inquired, eyes wide.

"Show-offs," Alice explained to her.

"Have you ever seen a contestant on a quiz show who didn't make a complete . . . uh . . . spectacle of himself?" Mike went on. "Now, don't tell me that before they get in front of the camera

15

they're all a bunch of shy, retiring introverts, but that once that red light goes on they all suddenly become cut-rate Uncle Milties. I don't believe it."

"Then, what you're saying is that all the TV quiz show producers are crooked?" Carol asked.

Mike looked slightly uncertain. "No, I'm just saying that, when choosing contestants, they're highly selective."

Carol addressed the children and Alice. "Now, *that* is a euphemism," she told them. Then she headed for the exit again. "Coming, Mike?"

"Anyway," Mike assured Alice and the children, backing away, "you won't see us on 'Stunts & Stumpers.' I have no intention of making a public spectacle of myself." He turned and followed Carol from the room.

"Well, we'll see," Alice murmured.

"What does that mean?" Peter asked, following Tiger as the dog loped toward its favorite resting place on the other side of the room.

"It comes from something Confucius said," Alice replied.

Peter halted and turned toward her. "Who he?"

"A Chinese philosopher. Sort of an early Charlie Chan," she answered. "He said: Man who go out door with mind made up better watch out or come back home with year's supply of pipe cleaners."

"Did he know Mike?" Cindy asked.

"Like an open book . . . like an open book . . ." Alice nodded.

In the car, driving at a leisurely pace toward

the city, Mike and Carol were quiet, both deep in thought. The freeway was not especially crowded. The lights of approaching cars looked like twin sets of meteors, suddenly flaring to brightness in the evening dimness, blazing intensely when they were almost upon the car, then suddenly disappearing, going black, as if they had burned themselves out completely.

Carol sighed all of a sudden—a happy sigh— and moved closer to Mike and slipped her arm through his, then rested her head on his shoulder.

"That could be dangerous," he said. "You're distracting me."

"Oh, pooh, you're a good driver, and there's hardly any traffic."

"I don't mean that," he smiled. "I mean I might get the idea that you're flirting with me and turn around and drive back home."

Carol laughed. "No chance," she said. "Not as eager as you are to see 'Stunts & Stumpers.'"

"Yeah, that's right, I am kind of hooked on that show."

"Mike. . . ."

"Mmmmmmmm?"

"I'm amazed," Carol said. "I really am. It's working out even better than I hoped." She sat up and turned in the seat, facing him. "Don't you think so?"

"Well, if I had some idea of what you're talking about . . ."

"The family, the bunch, I mean. We're getting along beautifully. Oh, there was that misunder-

17

standing between Tiger and Fluffy at the wedding, but—"

Mike had thrown back his head and was laughing heartily.

"What's that about?"

"Tiger and Fluffy . . . the whole thing. I just happened to be watching your Uncle Fred and Aunt Martha when the cat went flying across their laps, and then, right after it, the dog. They looked like they'd been told that there's really no Wall Street. But then, right on the dog's heels, came Greg and Marcia and Jan and Peter and Bobby and Cindy." He laughed again. "We're lucky they sent the wedding present before the wedding. If they'd had a chance to think it over, later, welllll . . ."

"Oh, you're exaggerating. I talked to them later and by then they'd decided it was hilarious —just what the occasion needed to give it the proper slant. But, since then, I mean. We've all meshed so well, don't you think?"

"Perfectly," Mike nodded.

"Well, nothing's perfect. But, considering, I think it's all worked out *very* well."

Mike glanced at her. "Considering what?"

"Oh, nothing. Except that you are all males, you know. And the male, by nature, does not domesticate as quickly and easily as the female. Anybody knows that."

"I was beginning to suspect that it was the other way around—in our case, that is," Mike replied.

Carol peered at him closely to see if he was joking. He wasn't, she decided. "What makes you say that?" she asked, concern in her tone.

"Well . . . I hadn't planned on mentioning it. I assumed it would pass. But, since you brought it up—this meshing . . . this getting-along-together . . . maybe it's my imagination, but I get the idea every now and then that the girls are working at it."

Carol smiled, relieved. "Of course they are," she replied. "A pleasant relationship doesn't just happen. We're all different, we're all individuals, and, if we're going to get along together, we have to make an effort."

Mike glanced at her again, a little hostilely this time. "I didn't realize it was such a struggle for you," he said.

"Mike!" Carol laughed. "I didn't say anything about a struggle."

He shrugged. "Okay."

"Well, as you say, since the subject *has* come up," Carol said, a hint of a chill in her tone. "I notice that the boys sometimes bend over backwards to keep the peace."

"Naturally. They're aware of their responsibility."

"Is *that* what it is?" Carol said coolly. "You make it sound like a super secret government project, which, if it fails, will totally destroy the civilized world—as we know it, of course."

Mike grinned. "Yeah, I guess I did," he said. He reached out and put his arm around her and drew her to him.

"Hey! That's dangerous!" Carol laughed, snuggling close to him.

"Don't worry—I'm a good driver and there's hardly any traffic. I have that on the best authority."

"I didn't mean that," she smiled. "I meant I might get the idea that you're flirting with me and grab the wheel from you and turn the car around and drive straight back home."

2.

When they reached the city, Mike drove the car to the neighborhood of the theater from which "Stunts & Stumpers" was televised and parked it in a public garage. Then he and Carol walked to the theater itself, which was only a little over a block away. There was a short line outside when they arrived, but it was moving, so before long they were inside the theater.

"Go right on in, please," an usher urged.

Mike looked at his watch. "It's still almost twenty minutes before the show starts," he replied.

"We're warming you up inside," the usher advised him.

"I'm not cold."

"I mean we've got a comic inside and he's telling jokes to get you in a good mood," the usher explained. "If you're not in a good mood, you won't laugh later when Jackie Jackson says something funny."

"Why not?" Mike asked, puzzled. "If it's funny, I'll laugh."

"That's why we have to get you in a good mood first," the usher explained. "Anything funny Jackie Jackson says, it isn't funny. Look," he said, lowering his voice, "I'm working my way through brain surgery school doing this, so, as a favor to me, would you just go inside and let the comic get you in a good mood? It won't hurt a bit."

"Yes, let's," Carol urged.

"But, darling, we'd be contributing to the perpetration of a fraud," Mike said. "If the good mood we're in when the audience at home sees us on the screen is artificial, then we're aiding and abetting the producer in creating the illusion that the program is enjoyable and we're having a good time. When, in fact—"

"Guy—" the usher interrupted. "Do us all a favor, huh? Stay out here for the whole show. If you go inside there with ideas like that, and it's catching, you could turn the whole studio into a funeral scene." He left Carol and Mike and fixed his attention on another couple that had entered the lobby.

"He's right, in a way, Mike," Carol said. "We *are* here to enjoy ourselves."

"But genuinely," Mike replied. "When it's about time for the show to start, we'll go in. Then," he added grimly, "let's see them make us laugh."

Carol giggled.

"It's the principle of the thing," Mike insisted. He looked at his watch again. "Twelve minutes to go."

Carol sighed resignedly. She glanced here and there about the lobby. Other people were moving quickly from the entranceway into the studio, urged along by ushers. Then, standing alone near a doorway at the far left of the lobby, she saw a small, middle-aged man who seemed vaguely familiar. She stared at him, trying to recall exactly where she had seen him before. He was wearing a conservative suit and conservative tie and severe British oxfords. Was he a diplomat? But, off hand, she couldn't remember even meeting any diplomats. He had a slightly shifty look about the eyes. Was he a loan officer at some bank? She couldn't recall the last time she had borrowed money though.

Then the man began staring back at her.

Carol smiled fleetingly and faced away from him—but not completely; she kept him within the range of the corner of her left eye. And good thing! A few seconds later, he left the doorway and approached the spot where she and Mike were standing, and he did not halt until he was within approximately three yards of them.

"Pssst!" the man hissed.

Startled, Carol turned and glared at him icily, then faced completely away from him.

"Psssst!"

"Mike!" Carol whispered, "there's a man hissing at me."

Mike looked at her, surprised, then raised his eyes and looked past her. "The one who looks like a crooked bank president?" he asked.

"Loan officer," she corrected. "And yes."

"He's motioning," Mike told her. "He's wagging his finger at us. He wants us for something."

"Ignore him," Carol said. "He's up to no good. People who go 'psssst!' in lobbies—or anywhere —are always up to no good. He probably wants to sell you something he stole."

"Let's find out," Mike said. "That, at least, would be a slice of real life—better than perpetrating a fraud in the interests of a phony quiz show." Taking Carol with him, with a hand on her arm, he walked toward where the man was still standing.

"Yes?" Mike asked.

"I'm sorry I didn't walk right up to you," the man replied, keeping his voice low. "I like to stay in the background. I didn't want anybody to see me and recognize me." He looked around warily. "I'm Jackie Jackson," he announced.

Carol hooted loudly—and then cringed, realizing how she had sounded. She was no more shocked than the strange man, however. He looked as if he wished he could curl up into a small ball and roll away.

"I'm sorry," Carol said, forcibly subduing herself, "but I have *seen* this show. And *you* are *not* Jackie Jackson. Jackie Jackson is tall and young and has seventy million teeth, each and every one a pearl, and he's a bundle of fun. I'll tell you one

24

thing for sure, he doesn't stand around in lobbies wagging his finger and going 'psssst! pssst! pssst!' "

"That's Jackie Jackson the personality you're talking about," the man replied. "At the moment, I'm Jackie Jackson the husband, father and home-owner, and—in my business capacity—the talent-judger."

"Uh-huh," Carol said dubiously. "And you took one look at me and said, 'Now, *there* is a zam-bam powerhouse of talent if I ever saw it, and I'll bet I can sell her husband on signing her up for a course at my private school of dramatics,' —right?"

"Lady, if you made a list of all the things I thought, what you just said wouldn't even make last place," the man replied. "What I thought, when I saw you both, was, 'Now, there's a nice looking couple, with not one ounce of phony talent between them.' "

Carol shrugged and turned to Mike. "Well, he *does* look a little familiar," she said. "Maybe he *is* Jackie Jackson."

The man waggled a finger at them again, then led them into the backstage area of the studio. He stopped a businesslike-looking young lady who was hustling past and asked her to identify him to Mike and Carol as Jackie Jackson. She did.

"*Mr. Jackson!*" Carol said excitedly. "This is such a thrill! I've seen you on television!"

"Fine, fine," Jackson replied, seemingly intimidated by her enthusiasm. "Now, uh, it's getting kind of late, so if I could just get your okay to be on the show . . . okay?"

"It's all right with me," Mike replied. "But why do you need our permission? I understand you've been on this show all season, and you've never had to ask us for an okay before."

Jackson looked at him glumly. "For *you* to be on the show," he explained. "This is how I pick the contestants. I stand out front and when I see a couple that looks like a typical pair of quiz show contestants—"

"Typical how?" Carol broke in. "Unbearable exhibitionists, you mean?"

Jackson shook his head. "Sometimes that happens later," he replied. "But they're not that way when I pick them. What I mean is, a nice, wholesome-looking couple. Just by looking at them, you can tell they have a whole houseful of kids and maybe a couple of pets—you know the kind. I've already picked two pair like that for tonight's show. You're the third. So—okay?"

"No, sorry," Mike replied.

"Oh, let's do!" Carol said. We might win something."

Mike shook his head. "No, I'm sorry, but I refuse to make a public spectacle of myself in return for a prize that I could get much easier by buying a box of Cracker Jacks."

"Hey!" Jackson protested. "Don't run down the prizes. You know what we're featuring tonight? A barrel of smoked salmon."

Carol's eyes opened wide. "A whole barrel? Free?"

"Not *entirely* free," Jackson replied. "Actually, what we're giving is a coupon for a discount."

"Sorry again—not interested," Mike said.

"Mike, the children would love it, seeing us on television," Carol pleaded. "Please? For their sakes?"

"Carol, don't try to use the children. They would probably be mortified. Especially after what I said just before we left about people who appear on television quiz shows."

"That's okay," Jackson said to Carol. "I understand how your husband feels. A lot of people are afraid of what can happen. I don't blame him a bit. It could be very embarrassing."

Mike peered at him suspiciously. "What do you mean, 'what could happen'? What *could* happen?"

"Well, sometimes people like you, people who are a little stuf— ah, not exactly stuffy. Reserved, let's say. People like that are afraid to relax. They think they might inadvertently reveal their inner selves. You'd be amazed what a lot of people who look very nice and wholesome on the outside are really like on the inside." He shuddered. Then, addressing Carol again, he said, "Like I say, I really don't blame your husband."

"But he's very nice both inside and outside," she replied.

Jackson smiled sympathetically. "Sure."

"I am!" Mike insisted.

"Okay, okay, okay—if you say so," Jackson answered, backing away. "Of course, saying it is one thing, and proving it is another, but—"

27

"We'll be on the show," Mike told him grimly. "I am *not* afraid of revealing my inner self."

"Now, that's courage!" Jackson said, impressed. He got Mike and Carol by the arm and hustled them along a corridor. "You'll be on last," he told them. "In fact, you might not even get on, you know. It's possible for one couple to keep going on this show forever—if they answer all the questions right and the sponsors keep renewing the show. But, so far, that hasn't happened. We had one couple that kept it up for a whole month once. But, unless I'm wrong, nobody has been on forever yet."

"How do you explain that?" Mike asked dryly.

"The questions get harder the longer the couple is on," Jackson replied. They had reached a door marked "Private," and he opened it and shooed Mike and Carol into a small room that was sparsely decorated and furnished with two lounge chairs, a couch, a coffee table and what looked like a television set. "That's a monitor," Jackson told them. "In a couple of minutes, the show will come on and you'll see it on it. How often do you see the show? Do you know how the game is played?"

"I *never* see the show," Mike told him proudly.

"Oh, I see it every chance I get," Carol said.

"No kidding? You know how we play it, then."

"Uh . . . well, I might be a little, uh . . . you see, I don't get a lot of chances to watch it. Usually, I'm doing something else."

"Okay, don't worry about it," Jackson said.

"Watch the show on the monitor. You'll hear me explain the game to the other couples. In fact, I use up most of the show explaining the game."

"That's show biz," Mike smiled.

"Yeah." He moved toward the door. "When it's about time for you to be on, somebody will come and get you," he said. "In the meantime—" His manner changed. He suddenly looked as if he realized, too late, that picking Mike and Carol to be on the show would prove to be the most terrible mistake of his whole life. "—don't be nervous," he said. Then he departed, closing the door behind him.

Mike put a hand to his forehead and closed his eyes, as if in severe pain. "This is preposterous! Let's get out of here!"

"Mike! We promised! What would they do if it came time for us to be on and we weren't anywhere around? The show might have to go off the air!"

"Honey, this country has been good to me—I'm willing to do that much in return for it," Mike replied. "Let's do it. Let's run out on 'Stunts & Stumpers' and destroy it for once and all."

"Oh, quit it." She sat down in one of the chairs, facing the monitor. A commercial was on. She looked at her watch. "This must be the station break," she said. "Come on, dear—watch. It'll be on in just a second."

Mike settled in the other chair and gave his attention to the screen. "Well, maybe we'll get lucky," he said. "Maybe the first couple will be bright and they'll go on and on and on, answering question after question after question, on into eternity."

"That's practically forever," Carol mused, distracted. She suddenly sat up straight, excited. "Here it comes!"

There was a blare of sound, meant to be a fanfare, from the monitor. Then, to a roar of applause, Jackie Jackson came bounding into view on the screen. He was suddenly young and tall and had seventy million teeth, each and every one a pearl, and a bundle of fun. The audience went wild cheering him. When he finally got them quieted down, he told everybody what had happened to him on the way to the studio. The laughter was deafening. Grown men and women fell out of their seats in fits of uncontrollable hilarity.

"I don't get it," Mike said to Carol, baffled.

"I get it," she replied, "but I don't really think it's *that* funny. After all, a lot of men stop and buy a newspaper on their way to work."

A few seconds later, the first contestants were herded into view by a pretty girl, who then disappeared and was never seen or heard from again. The man and woman were middle aged and well dressed. They were both smiling nervously.

"Wholesome," Mike said. "Do we look like that?"

"There are different ways of looking wholesome," Carol replied defensively.

Jackie Jackson explained the game to the couple, a Mr. and Mrs. Hackemore. Mr. Hackemore would be given a stunt to perform. If, in the opinion of the audience, he accomplished it satisfactorily, he and Mrs. Hackemore would then each be given a category and begin answering questions in those categories. As long as they both answered the questions correctly they would continue as contestants—and would continue receiving prizes. But if one missed a question, then both would be eliminated.

"Oh, boy!" Jackie Jackson smirked, "I can just imagine the kind of trouble that could cause, can't you, Mr. and Mrs. Hackemore? I mean, suppose Mrs. Hackemore answers her question correctly and Mr. Hackemore answers his *in*correctly! Wowee! Mrs. Hackemore will be furious, won't she! Why, the last couple we had on the show went directly from the studio to their lawyer's office to start divorce proceedings! Wowee!"

Again, the members of the audience exploded in laughter, and, once more, the camera picked up shots of adult men and women rolling in the aisles, overcome by mirth—yet, somehow, still able to wave to the folks at home.

"Ain't we a devil!" Jackie Jackson asked the Hackemores rhetorically.

"Only in the sense that you belong somewhere underground," Mike replied, addressing the comment to the monitor.

"Shhhh!" Carol said.

Jackie Jackson was telling Mr. Hackemore what his stunt would be. Mr. Hackemore was to try to push a peanut a whole block, using only his

31

nose. At the mere mention of this, the audience erupted again in a roar of laughter.

Mike touched his fingers to the tip of his nose. "That's criminal," he said emphatically.

"It's just a stunt," Carol said. "Didn't you ever push a peanut with your nose when you were a child?"

"Yes. There was a time in my life when I wore a bib, too. But, since then, I've grown up."

"Shhhh—watch!"

A camera followed Jackie Jackson and Mr. Hackemore out of the theater and then to the end of the block. There, an assistant supplied Mr. Hackemore with a peanut. Mr. Hackemore dropped it to the sidewalk; then, encouraged (bullied) by Jackie Jackson, he got down on his hands and knees and began propelling it along the cement with the tip of his nose. Every once in a while, he and the peanut were replaced on the screen by shots of the audience. Little old ladies, reduced to unconsciousness by laughter, were regularly being carried out on stretchers.

The peanut, trailed by Mr. Hackemore, finally reached the end of the block. Mr. Hackemore rose, then was whisked offscreen. When he re-appeared, back inside the studio and onstage, his nose was heavily bandaged. He grinned gamely, however. And the applause he received shook the whole building.

"If Jackson even *mentions* the word peanut to me—" Mike began.

"Shhh—the questions are starting!"

"Mrs. Hackemore," Jackie Jackson beamed,

32

"your category is: Transportation. And now, for a year's supply of pipe cleaners, here's your first question: On his famous midnight gallop, Paul Revere was riding—a what, Mrs. Hackemore? Tell me what Paul Revere was riding."

Mrs. Hackemore looked terribly pained. "Golly . . . I know it's a trick question . . ."

"Think, Mrs. Hackemore," Jackson urged.

"Gee!" Carol said, annoyed. "I know that—it's right on the tip of my tongue."

"It's what!" Mike said, appalled. "You mean you don't know?"

"Mrs. Hackemore . . . time is running out . . ." Jackson said. "I'll give you a hint—it's an animal."

"A coati-mundi!" Mrs. Hackemore squealed.

"Oh, Mrs. Hackemore!" Jackson replied, deeply disappointed. "That was close . . . but not quite it. The answer is: a horse. Too bad, Mrs. Hackemore," he said, showing all of his seventy million teeth, meanwhile moving the couple offscreen, "but better luck next time!" He faced the audience. "How about a big hand—"

The words that followed were drowned out by a holocaust of whistling, stamping and yelling.

"Coati-mundi!" Mike said disgustedly. "Boy, I hope we get easy questions like that."

"Well . . . I thought it was a trick question, too—I sympathize with her," Carol said.

"I sympathize with *him!*" Mike said. "Did you see that nose? Yiii! He'll be wearing it in a sling for the next six months."

"Here comes the next couple," Carol said.

33

The man and wife, Mr. and Mrs. Fullminster, were introduced to the audience. Then Mr. Fullminster was given his stunt to perform. Off-stage, he changed into a bathing suit. When he reappeared he was blindfolded, then made to walk a plank. At the end of it he dropped into a tank of water twelve-feet-deep. While the audience was rolling in the aisles, Mrs. Fullminster casually mentioned to Jackie Jackson that Mr. Fullminster was not much of a swimmer. After Mr. Fullminster was located at the bottom of the tank and was revived—to tumultuous applause —the questioning began.

"Mrs. Fullminster, your category is: Our Flowery Friends. Now, for a year's supply of pipe cleaners, here is your first question: When the man got up from the chair, what he did was also the name of a flower. What flower, Mrs. Fullminster?"

Mrs. Fullminster scowled deeply, thinking.

"Nasturtium!" Carol blurted out.

"What!" Mike said. "You're kidding!"

"Columbine?" Carol guessed meekly.

Then Mrs. Fullminster gave her answer. "Rose," she said. "When the man got up from the chair, he rose. Rose is the answer."

"That is correct. Mrs. Fullminster!" Jackie Jackson shouted, bursting with admiration and exultation. "Audience—let's hear it for Mrs. Fullminster!"

Pandemonium.

"Shucks . . . sure . . . the rose," Carol said, disappointed in herself. "Why didn't I think of that?" She sighed woefully. "Oh, Mike, I'm going to be terrible. I don't know a thing. I'm going to make a complete fool of myself."

"Cheer up," he replied. "We probably won't even get on."

The door opened and an usher appeared. He asked Mike and Carol to follow him, then led them toward the wings.

"In case there's time for you to go on," the usher explained to them, "we want you to be right there, waiting."

"That makes sense," Mike nodded.

"Oh, Mike, how can you be so calm?" Carol asked, clutching his arm. "I'm a nervous wreck, and we're not even anywhere *near* a camera. Mike . . . Mike, if I have to go out there and face that audience, I'll be sick."

"Nonsense," he laughed. "As I understand it, you don't even see the audience. The lights are in your eyes. The whole studio will look deserted. The only way you'll know there are people out there will be when you hear the applause."

"They won't applaud for me," she said, miserable. "I'll be so dumb."

"Honey, the people in that audience would applaud an unintentional pause."

They reached the wings and the usher signaled for them to halt. From where they had stopped they could see Jackie Jackson and Mr. and Mrs. Fullminster on stage.

"And now, Mr. Fullminster, here is your first question in your category," Jackie Jackson advised the husband. "Ready? Here goes: We all know, of course, that, in religion, modernism was the movement that was intended to reconcile the developments of nineteenth-century science and philosophy with historic Christianity, and that it began with the evident disparity between Darwin's theory of evolution and the old literal interpretation of Genesis. That's common knowledge. But, what everybody does *not* know is who it was who influenced modernism by philosophical attempts to read Darwinian principles into the history of non-spiritual civilization. Mr. Fullminster, give me the name of that person."

Mr. Fullminster looked stunned.

"Oh, boy, I bet he wishes he was still at the bottom of that tank!" Carol said. "I mean, nobody knows the answer to that!"

"You're not serious," Mike replied. "That's as easy as the question about Paul Revere's coatimundi."

Carol looked up at him speculatively. "Then what's the answer?"

"Herbert Spencer. You mean you really didn't know?"

Carol stared at him, awe-struck.

Mike pointed toward the stage. "Listen—I think Fullminster has it," he said.

She turned her attention back to the action just as Mr. Fullminster hazarded a wild guess.

"Mickey Mantle?" Mr. Fullminster murmured.

"I'm sorry," Jackie Jackson said, suddenly shaken to the depths by remorse. "Gee . . . I thought you'd get that one. It was so *easy*. But, no, the answer isn't Mickey Mantle, Mr. Fullminster—it's Herbert Spencer."

Mike nodded agreement.

"What team is he on?" Carol asked him.

"He was a British philosopher," Mike told her.

"But, how—"

The audience was going mad with emotion again, applauding the departure of Mr. and Mrs. Fullminster.

As the couple entered the wings, Mrs. Fullminster began deriding her husband for his abysmal ignorance. "Mickey Mantle!" she screeched. "You should have known it wasn't him when you didn't understand the question!"

"And now let's have our next couple!" Jackie Jackson shouted gleefully.

"Mike! I can't go on!" Carol cried out in panic.

"Honey, it's nothing," Mike assured her. Then, smiling his most winning smile, he escorted her out onto the stage.

3.

At the Brady house, Alice, Marcia, Greg, Jan, Peter, Cindy and Bobby sat staring vacantly at the television screen, crushed under the weight of disappointment, as Mr. and Mrs. Fullminster made their way from the spotlight and the camera panned across the audience.

"Let's face it," Alice said. "They decided to go somewhere else or they lost the tickets on the way in or they forgot to take the tickets with them or they're hiding under those two seats in the far corner of the studio."

"They're not under the seats," Peter said. "That's where those two little old ladies were sitting who were carried out on stretchers."

"Well, they're not there, that's for sure," Alice said. "I've seen that audience so often, every face in it is an old friend. Let's switch channels and get something interesting."

"It wath interesthting when that man thtayed in the water tho long," Cindy said. "Maybe he'll do it again. I like it when he pourth water out of hith earth."

"His ears are probably dry by now, so—" Alice began.

"Look!" Marcia suddenly cried. "It's them!"

Alice blinked at the screen. Mike and Carol had appeared. They were standing at either side of the m.c., Jackie Jackson. Carol was smiling brightly at the audience. And Mike was looking like a lump, as if he had suddenly had a spell cast upon him.

The children collected close to the screen, all shouting for the others to be quiet.

"Stop shouting 'Be Quiet!' and be quiet!" Alice shouted.

Peter dragged Tiger up to the screen. "See?" he said. "It's them! They're on! See?"

Tiger squirmed out of his grasp and trotted back to his favorite resting place.

"He's a cynic," Greg told Peter, referring to the dog. "Anything he can't smell, he doesn't believe in."

"Please!" Alice begged. "Let's listen. Shhhh-hhhh!"

"Well, hi, folks," Jackson said, grinning broadly, as the applause for Mike's and Carol's entrance died down. "Say, you're a handsome couple!" He faced the audience again. "Aren't they a handsome couple?"

Again, the theater shook from the enthusiastic response.

"All right, now, handsome couple," Jackson

beamed, specifically addressing Mike, "let's have your name. You're Mr. and Mrs.—"

Mike continued to stare glassily into space, struck numb by an acute case of stage fright.

Jackson made urging motions with his hands, trying to help Mike. "Mr. and Mrs.—Mr. and Mrs. What?"

"Yeah, yeah," Mike nodded, suddenly coming to life. "Mr. and Mrs. What."

Carol whooped. "Isn't that *won*derful!" she hooted. "He's like that *all* the time—a real card!" Whereas being in the spotlight seemed to have turned Mike off, it appeared to have turned Carol on. She looked like someone who had had an overdose of laughing gas. "And you ought to hear him when he's his real self," she told the audience. "I mean when he's *real*ly sharp and can remember his own name! Wheeeeee!"

"Ah . . . yah," Jackson said, temporarily cowed by Carol's bubbly effusiveness. "But . . . ah, now, if we could just get the name . . ."

"Brady's the name and homemaking's the game," Carol replied, winking broadly. "I'm Carol Brady, and this handsome, bright-eyed fellow over here—" She punched Mike, then winked to the audience again. "—pay attention, boy, I'm talking to you! This handsome fellow is my husband, Mr. Mike Brady."

The applause rose again—whether for Carol or for Mike, it was not clear.

"Well, Mr. Brady," Jackson said, turning to Mike, "what business are you in?"

Mike's eyes rolled ceilingward as he tried desperately to recall what he did when he went to work each day.

"Architect," Carol said, answering for him. "Isn't that interesting? People always say that to me when I tell them I'm married to an architect. They always say: 'Isn't that interesting!' And, you know, they're right." She stepped forward, getting a pace closer to the audience, planting herself between the camera and Jackie Jackson. "I think a lot of us tend to think that all there is to architecture is designing houses and buildings," she told the audience, becoming sober and sincere. "But, believe me, there's a *lot* more to it than that. For instance, Mike and I have six children. Oh, yes, I know, you're saying, 'Her? So young? So attractive?' But, of course, the truth is that we don't actually have six children all together. I mean, I have three, all girls. And Mike has three, all boys. And then there's the dog and the cat."

"And me," Alice reminded her from the living room at home.

"And Alice," Carol went on. "Alice is a jewelllll! Honest. But then, you don't want to hear about Alice, you want to hear about architecture."

"Give them a chance!" Alice protested. "How do you know? Maybe they're dying to hear about Alice!"

"Architecture—" Carol said, advancing another step on the camera.

"Well, that *is* interesting!" Jackie Jackson broke in, reaching out and getting Carol by the

41

elbow and easing her back into line beside him. "Isn't that interesting, folks!" he called out. "Let's hear it for architecture!"

The applause was thunderous.

At home, Greg faced the others, perplexed. "What's going on?" he wanted to know. "She's hogging the whole camera. Dad hasn't had a chance to say a word."

"Chance?" Marcia protested. "He's had all the *chance* in the world. He just isn't a personality, that's all. He can't even remember his own name."

"She didn't give him a chance!" Greg insisted.

"All right, all right," Alice said soothingly. "It isn't a screen test, you know. Now, just watch . . . watch . . ."

The applause had tapered off.

"Are you ready, Mr. Brady?" Jackie Jackson beamed. "It's *that* time—time for your stunt. Now, here's what we're going to do. We're going to— ah . . . Mr. Brady . . . can you hear me? Are you listening?"

Mike gazed blankly at Carol.

"Nod your head, dear," she told him.

Mike nodded.

"He understands," Carol told Jackie Jackson. "Isn't it interesting," she said, stepping toward the camera again, "how a simple gesture such as a nod of the head can convey so much meaning. There's a lesson for all of us in that, I think, in this age of credibility gaps and generation gaps. It's so often said that the problem is communication. Or, to put it another way, a *lack* of communication. Now, of course, there isn't a lot that can be said with a simple nod of the head. On the other head, though—that is, on the other *hand*, though—we're often told that we need to get back to basics. And how much more basic can communications get than a simple nod of the—"

Carol was interrupted by a thunderous burst of applause. Puzzled, she looked back, and saw that Jackie Jackson was holding up a sign that said: APPLAUSE!

Defeated, Carol stepped back into line, taking her place beside him. Jackson then held up a second sign, saying: SHUT UP!

The applause ended instantly and the studio became completely still.

"As I was saying, Mr. Brady," Jackson went on, addressing Mike again, "it's time for your stunt. What we want you to do, Mr. Brady, is use your imagination. You *do* have an imagination, don't you?"

"Does he have an imagination!" Carol began. "Let me tell—"

"Wonderful! Wonderful! Wonderful!" Jackie Jackson shouted, drowning her out. "Okay," he said, speaking to Mike once more, "here's what we're going to do." He led Mike to one end of the stage to a kitchen-type chair. "We're going to ask you to sit on this chair, Mr. Brady. Do you think you can manage that?"

Mike looked panic-stricken.

"Sit!" Carol ordered.

"Fine," Jackie Jackson smiled, as Mike lowered himself to the seat of the chair. "And now we're going to tie your hands behind your back and to the chair." An assistant, using cord, began tying Mike's arms behind him. "Good, good, Mr. Brady," Jackie Jackson complimented him, "you're doing very well, sitting there all alone while the young man ties you up. Now, look across the stage, Mr. Brady, to the other side. No, no, over there—that's the other side. This is this side. Got that? Okay—see that telephone over there? Wonderful—you see it. Fine, now, Mr. Brady—here's your stunt. What we want you to do is imagine that you've been tied to this chair by a burglar. Got that? And the burglar escaped with all your money. Now, Mr. Brady, we want you to figure out how to get across the stage to the telephone and call the police. You have five minutes to do it. Simple? Okay, Mr. Brady— Go!"

As Jackie Jackson moved away from Mike, leaving him alone on the chair, the children and Alice crowded closer to the television set at home, as if they believed that if the worst came to the worst they would be able to rush onto the screen and snatch him away from the mocking eyes of the audience.

Mike was scowling, evidently thinking.

"Don't worry," Jan said to the boys. "Any idiot could figure that out."

"Sure, all he has to do is call for Superman," Bobby said. "Any idiot knows that."

"Don't forget—he's under a lot of pressure," Alice said. "He's up there on that stage and all those bright lights are on him and all those people are watching him. It's not like being home in

44

your own chair. A lot of people get stage fright."

"Mom didn't," Marcia said.

"She did, too," Greg said. "She just got it in reverse. She doesn't babble like that around here, does she?"

"She wasn't babbling," Marcia replied indignantly, "she was sparkling!"

"Sparkling! Boy—"

"Watch!" Alice ordered.

Mike was showing signs of recovering. He was trying to separate his hands by breaking the cord.

"Not that way!" Greg shouted to him. "Scoot the chair! Scoot the chair over to the phone!"

"That's cheating!" Marcia objected. "You're telling him how! No coaching from the audience!"

"I'm not the audience!" Greg replied.

"Oh, no!" Alice cried. "Stop!" she bellowed at the screen.

Mike was bouncing the chair up and down, tugging at the cords, and it was carrying him toward the edge of the stage.

"Back! Back!" Alice waved.

"He can't hear you!" Greg told her.

Alice leaped up and ran to a window and threw it up and shrieked into the night. "Stop! Back! Back! Stop!"

"It's okay," Peter called to her. "He must have heard you. He stopped bouncing."

Alice closed the window and hurried back to the television set. Mike was resting, scowling deeply again, evidently thinking once more.

"He'll figure it out now," Greg said, confident.

"Why don't we call him and tell him how," Bobby said.

"Boy, dumb," Greg replied irritably. "How do you expect him to get to a phone?"

"There's one right there on the other side of the television picture," Bobby pointed.

"He'll never in a million years get to *that* phone," Jan said. Then she giggled.

"How old do you have to be to hit a girl?" Peter asked Alice.

"A lot older than—oh-oh! Oh, that's a shame," Alice said, looking sadly at the screen. "They didn't give him a full five minutes, did they? That's *really* a shame. He would have figured it out."

On the screen, the assistant was untying Mike's hands. When he had him free, Jackie Jackson escorted him back to where Carol was waiting.

"I almost had it," Mike said apologetically to Carol. "A couple more minutes and I would have had my hands loose."

"All you had to do, darling," she replied, speaking directly into the camera, "was scoot the chair across the floor."

"I'm over here," Mike said to her. "I'm not in the camera."

Jackie Jackson intervened. "Whattayasay, folks?" he called out, addressing the audience. "He did his best, didn't he? Shall we give it to him?"

Again, the building trembled, as the audience responded with a roar of approval.

But Mike was shaking his head. "No, I couldn't accept that," he said. "I lost . . . I accept the consequences."

The audience groaned.

"He accepts the consequences, folks!" Jackie Jackson said joyfully. "And the consequences is: we give it to him. He completed his stunt, so now we go on to—to what?"

"The stumpers!" the audience shrieked.

"Well, you heard it," Jackie Jackson said to Mike and Carol. "Now, I want you each to pick a category." He pointed to a large board at the back of the stage where the possibilities were listed. "Make it easy on yourself. You know what you know best, so—"

"I'll take Number Five—Trivia!" Carol said.

"Mrs. Brady picks Number Five—Trivia!" Jackie Jackson announced to the audience.

There was pandemonium! Several more little old ladies, overcome by the emotional wrench that Carol's decision had given them, were carried out on stretchers.

"I'll . . . uh, take, uh . . . Number Seven —Architecture," Mike informed Jackson.

"Wonderful! Mr. Brady, folks, will take— ahhh, Mr. Brady, Number Seven is Ancient Greek Literature. Number Three is Architecture. Which will it be?"

"He'll pick Number Three," Carol said. "He's an architect. So, naturally, that would be the easiest category for him. It ought to be a snap."

"Yes, that's right," Mike said dimly. "I'll take Number Seven—Ancient Greek Literature. I'm an ancient Greek. So, naturally, that ought to be the best category for me. It'll be a snap."

"Darling—" Carol began.

"Sorry, Mrs. Brady, but he made his choice," Jackie Jackson said. "It's Number Seven—Ancient Greek Literature."

"But—"

"Let's hear it for Ancient Greek Literature, folks!" Jackson shouted, urging the audience to respond.

Once more there was stomping, screaming and whistling.

"That's class!" Jackson told the stompers, screamers and whistlers when they had finally quieted down. "I congratulate you, intellectuals. That's the biggest yell for Ancient Greek Literature we've ever had on this show!"

The stomping, screaming and whistling resumed.

"Well, Mrs. Brady, so you picked Trivia for your category, did you?" Jackie Jackson said, when the studio had become quiet again. "Any particular reason? Do you consider yourself a trivia expert?"

"Oh, no—no, no, no, no!" Carol bubbled. "That was my reason. Basically, you see, I'm not an expert on anything. I'm just . . . just dumb ol' me. And that's why I picked Trivia. Because trivia isn't anything, either. It's just a big ol' bunch of nothing. I'll tell you something very personal about yours truly. I'm—"

"Well, maybe we better not hear it," Jackson

broke in, looking a bit wary. "This is a family show. If it's something—"

"Oh, nooooooo! Nothing like that!" Carol replied, giggling. "What I was going to say is, I have a very strange mind."

"I was beginning to guess," Jackson nodded. "Now—"

"And what I mean by that, when I say I have a very strange mind," Carol went on, "is that I can never remember an important thing, but I never forget an *un*important thing. Isn't that strange? A lot of people tell me that. 'Carol,' they say, 'you've got a strange mind.' Because, for instance, I can never remember to turn the iron off after I've finished ironing, but I never forget Elsworth Oppenweiser's birthday. Isn't that strange?"

"Elsworth Oppenweiser?"

"He designed the first plastic toothpick."

"Okay, let's get on with the game," Jackie Jackson said. He got a number of small cards from his pocket. "Now—for a year's supply of pipe cleaners, Mrs. Brady—the first question in the Trivia category is: In the 1922 motion picture 'While Rome Burns,' two extras in the big conflagration scene were a couple of wiseacres who had slipped onto the set in bedsheets instead of togas to win a bet. Now . . . what were their names?"

"Oh, that's easy," Carol replied. "The tall one was Ronald Firebanker, and the short one was—talk about coincidences—Elsworth Oppenweiser, who, years later, was to design—"

"That's right!" Jackson shouted excitedly.

The audience broke into a fit of wild exultation again.

"I can also tell you a little bit about them," Carol said, when the applause had died down. "Ronald Firebanker, at that time, lived at 17906 Buena Noches Boulevard—although he was planning to move to a flat in the next block south the following Tuesday—and Elsworth Oppenweiser—"

"Thank you, thank you, thank you, Mrs. Brady, but the names are all we want." He turned to Mike. "Okay, Mr. Brady, here it goes. For a free spark plug check-up at Al's Service Station and 24-Hour Garage & Snackery, the first question in the Ancient Greek Literature category is:—"

"Julius Caesar," Mike said.

"Ahhhh . . . I haven't asked the question yet, Mr. Brady," Jackson told him.

"Julius Caesar was a Roman, anyway, darling," Carol said to Mike.

"Ah, ah, ah, ah, ah!" Jackson said, shaking his head. "Don't help him, Mrs. Brady. That would—"

There was a sudden loud honking sound.

"Oh, too bad, too bad!" Jackson said, sounding delighted.

"A horn!" Mike shouted, inspired. "That was a horn! Used by the ancient Greeks to . . . uh . . . to clear the traffic off the road!"

"That wasn't the question, either, Mr. Brady,"

Jackson advised him. "That was the signal that means we're out of time. We won't have time for a question in your category tonight, Mr. Brady, but, tell me— Will you and Mrs. Brady be back with us next week?" He was shaking his head hopefully.

"Why not?" Carol replied gaily. "After all, with a free spark plug check-up hanging in the balance—"

The studio band broke in with an eardrum-bursting rendition of the "Stunts & Stumpers" theme song, drowning her out. The audience erupted with cheers and screams. Several little old ladies, driven to a frenzy, began ripping seats out of the roots. Jackie Jackson, grinning cavernously, showing all seventy-million of his teeth, each and every one a pearl, waved with both hands to both the audience in the studio and the audience at home. Carol began throwing kisses to the studio audience, to the stagehands, to the technicians, to the cameramen, to the director, to the producer.

Mike just stood, sagging a little, looking wistful.

At the house, Alice switched off the television set. "To bed, everybody!" she ordered firmly.

"Let us stay up until Mike and Mom get home," Marcia begged. "I want to hear about it."

"You saw it—that's enough," Alice said.

"Seeing it was *too much*, if you ask me," Greg said, leaving the room.

Peter and Bobby hurried after him.

51

"I don't blame them for not wanting to hear about it," Marcia said to Alice, "but Mom was great, so *we* don't have to go to bed, do we?"

Alice pointed, stiff-armed, toward the doorway. "Go!"

Marcia, Jan and Cindy started to leave. Then Jan halted. "Alice, when they get home," she said, "you can tell Mike it's okay with us if he isn't a brilliant personality like Mom. Tell him he's still a great dad."

"When they get home," Alice said, "I'm going to do the kindest thing I can think off—keep my mouth shut. Now . . . good night."

4.

When Mike awakened the next morning, he lay in bed for a few minutes peering stonily up at the ceiling. Then he got up and stood in front of the mirror and stared at himself for a short while. Finally, he returned to the bed and shook Carol, waking her.

"I think I had a terrible nightmare last night," he said. "I want you to tell me it isn't really true. Did we—"

"We did," Carol replied.

Mike sat down on the edge of the bed and covered his face with his hands. "I'm disgraced. I did it. I made a public spectacle of myself. I'll never be able to look anybody in the eye again."

"Oh, Mike!" Carol laughed. "You're making too much of it. Just because you had a little touch of stage fright . . . you'll be a lot better next week."

Mike shuddered. "I *knew* it! That was the worst part of the nightmare. I saw myself promising Jackie Jackson I'd go back and make a public spectacle of myself again next week. I did it, didn't I?"

"Not exactly in those words," Carol replied. "You promised to go back again, though."

"He probably threatened me with a lawsuit to get me to promise, didn't he?"

"Uh . . . no . . . when the show ended, you told him you *wouldn't* be back. And he said he understood, that you were probably afraid of disgracing yourself in front of your children and business associates and friends and—"

Mike had removed his hands from his face and had turned and was peering at her questioningly. "Disgrace myself how?" he asked.

"Well . . . you sort of picked Ancient Greek Literature as a category and—"

"You know," he told her, "it just so happens that I minored in Greek lit in college. Of course," he admitted, "I don't remember *everything* I learned, but—"

"For one thing," Carol said, "you didn't remember that Julius Caesar wasn't a Greek."

"I couldn't think straight—that Jackson was honking a horn at me. It was right in my ear." He got up and headed for the shower. "Wait'll next week, though," he said. "I probably have my Greek lit textbooks somewhere. I'll do a little boning up, and—"

The door closed behind him.

Carol rose and went to the kitchen. The children were at the table, eating breakfast. Alice was pouring orange juice. The girls immediately bombarded Carol with questions about the television show. The boys engaged themselves in a discussion about the standing of the various baseball teams in the western divisions of the major leagues.

"You just sort of lighted up the whole screen, Mom," Marcia told Carol. "It was really exciting. Like a movie. You know, in the scene where the Little Miss Nobody all of a sudden becomes a Big Star."

"Really?" Carol smiled, pleased. "Frankly, I don't remember much about it. It's very strange. You—"

"Like your mind," Alice said.

"What?"

"Like your mind," she repeated. "You told us all that you have a very strange mind."

Carol's eyes opened wide. "I did?" She shrugged. "Well, if I did, I did, I suppose. I don't recall that at all. I remember what happened —in general—but I don't remember . . . well, lighting up the screen."

"Like a fireworks display," Alice told her.

Carol smiled again, even more pleased. "Is that so? Maybe I have a talent I didn't know about."

"I liked the part," Cindy said, "where the man poured water out of hith ear."

Mike entered the room at that moment. He was dressed for the office. As he joined the others at the table, they all became self-consciously silent. Mike smiled a good-morning, then sipped his orange juice. The good-mornings he got in response were uncommonly subdued. Puzzled, he looked around the table at the faces of the children. They were all busy eating, avoiding his gaze. Mike cleared his throat, finished off the orange juice, put the glass down, then commented on the agreeable state of the weather. In answer, the children nodded and murmured.

"I didn't really have a chance," Mike said to the children. "The program was over before I had an opportunity to say anything."

"No, you were great, Dad," Greg said. "Say, how about those Angels—they're really battling for that top spot in the league, aren't they?"

"Just wait'll next week," Mike replied.

"Who are they playing next week?"

"I'm not talking about the Angels, I'm talking about me," Mike said. "That free spark plug check-up is practically in the bag."

"Oh!" Greg said, looking surprised. "Are you talking about that quiz show? I'd forgotten all about that." He looked at the other boys. "You, too, right, guys?"

"Sure," Peter replied. "Anyway, Dad, a lot of people on those quiz shows act like dumbheads."

"Thanks," Mike replied.

"How could you forget about it?" Cindy said to Greg, baffled. "Don't you remember the man who poured water out of hith ear?"

Mike looked at his watch. "I'm a little late," he said, rising. "I'll have something sent in . . . or something . . . when I get to the office." He kissed Carol and waved feebly to Alice and the children, then departed.

"That was terrible!" Carol said.

56

"What could we say?" Greg replied defensively. "Anything we would have said about last night would have been wrong. I just thought it would be best not to talk about it. Anyway, what we did wasn't anything compared to what you did."

"What I did?" Carol responded. "What did I do?"

"You made him look like a dope," Peter told her.

"I did?"

"You couldn't help it, Mom," Marcia said. "A star can't dim its brilliance, can it? If a person is destined to be a shining light, what can a person do?"

Carol thought it over for a second. "I suppose there's a lot of truth to that," she admitted finally.

Shortly after breakfast ended, Carol began getting telephone calls. Her friends were phoning to congratulate her on her performance. The sixth call—from Maggie, the friend from whom she had received the tickets to Stunts & Stumpers—however, was for a different reason. Maggie was phoning to tell her that she was not speaking to her anymore.

Carol: Maggie! What do you mean? What did I do?

Maggie: You got on that program and you practically stole the whole show, that's what you did. Carol, it's been my life's ambition to be on "Stunts & Stumpers" and glitter like you did.

Carol: What do you mean, 'practically' stole the show. According to what everybody else says, I *did* steal it.

Maggie: Aha! You admit it. What I can't figure out is why I let you talk me out of those tickets in the first place.

Carol: Maggie, you called me and almost forced me to take them—remember? Is it my fault that Frank had to fly to Chicago all of a sudden on business? Believe me, honest, if the choice had been mine, that would have been you up there last night instead of me.

Maggie: How about next week? I could take your place.

Carol: I don't think the producer would allow it, Maggie. I did sort of, well, you know, make a hit with the audience. Producers have to worry about their rating. A 'name' on the show can mean the difference between—

Maggie: We wouldn't tell the producer. I'd just go and pretend to be you.

Carol: Maggie! You're six inches taller than I am and our hair is a different color and—

Maggie: I'll wear a wig!

Carol: I'm sorry, Maggie, but—oh, listen, I'll have to call you back. Mike just came in. He's supposed to be at the office. Something must have happened.

Maggie: Well . . . okay, if you call me. But don't expect me to call you. I'm not speaking to you anymore, remember.

Carol hung up and went to meet Mike. She

found him in his combination den and home office unloading a large pile of books.

"Hi!" Mike smiled.

"What happened?" she asked. "Why aren't you at the office?"

"Oh . . . well, I didn't quite get there," Mike replied. "I'll call them and tell them I can't make it today. I . . . uh . . . I stopped at the library." He indicated the books. "That's where I got those."

"Gee, what an unusual idea—is that what they're pushing these days—books?"

Mike laughed. "Well, I was driving by, and— actually, I remembered that I sold my Greek lit textbooks as soon as I finished the course. It wasn't the subject that interested me the most. So, I thought, if I wanted to brush up—" He indicated the books again. "They're on ancient Greek literature."

"I see," Carol replied coolly. "You don't consider that cheating?"

"Cheating?" Mike asked, surprised. "Studying is cheating? How do you think I got to be an architect? I studied."

"That is *entirely* different," she said. "You *wanted* to be an architect. But you just admitted that you've *never* had any genuine interest in ancient Greek literature. So, I don't know what you'd call it if it isn't cheating. You don't see *me* sitting around cramming, do you?"

"How could you cram on trivia?" Mike asked. "That's the kind of inconsequential junk you either remember or you don't."

59

"Junk!"

"Junk!" Mike repeated. "Who cares what two guys wandered onto the set of a 1922 movie in bedsheets? Even if you know it, what do you know? What can you do with information like that?"

"For one thing, you can glitter," Carol replied. "And that's a completely unbiased opinion. Maggie told me that. I was talking to her on the phone a few minutes ago, and that was her exact word —she told me I glittered on that screen."

"She was probably telling you your nose was shiny," Mike replied gruffly, picking up one of the books he had got at the library. "I can skip through these this afternoon and refresh my memory on some of the obscure shadings that have probably slipped my mind," he said, "and then maybe drop in at the office this evening and take care of anything important that's come up." He smiled tightly. "If you'll excuse me, Miss Glitter . . . this is deep stuff. It requires the utmost concentration."

Carol backed toward the doorway. "Mike, if I'd known you were going to be jealous, honest, I wouldn't have glittered."

"I'm not jealous," he assured her. "I just don't want to look like—as Peter so aptly put it—a 'dumbhead' again next week."

"Oh . . . well, okay . . ."

"I might do a little glittering myself," Mike said, opening the book he was holding and moving toward an easy chair. "A man who's both a scholar and a wit can attract a good deal of attention in the right setting."

"Scholar and wit?" Carol said, halting.

"You told me yourself recently that I have an incisive wit," Mike said, settling in the chair. "And a man who's an expert on ancient Greek literature certainly has to be classed as a scholar. So, putting one and one together, you get—"

"A scholar and a wit," Carol nodded. "What did you mean about the 'right setting'?"

"Well, put a scholar and wit in among a bunch of other scholars and wits, and what have you got? Nothing. None of them stands out. *But!* Put a scholar and wit in a setting where you expect to see a bunch of dumbheads, and then, obviously, you've got something a little different. Need I say more?"

Carol moved back into the room. "Mike, you're an architect," she said. "You're a great architect. You're—"

"I am not yet a great architect," Mike broke in, correcting her.

"But architecture is your thing," she told him. "You wouldn't be happy as a scholar and wit. Mike, believe me, glitter is not for you."

"Carol, if I'd known you were going to be jealous, honest, I wouldn't have brought these books home. I'd have gone to the office with them."

"Jealous! Whoooo!"

Carol turned and marched from the room. She

swung the door closed behind her, then stood glaring into space.

Alice came along and stopped and studied Carol. Then she looked at the closed door. "Will he be sleeping in there, too?" she asked.

"What? Oh . . . no . . . only cheating." Carol's glare became even more severe. "You know what sauce for the gander is also sauce for?" she said.

"Goose?"

"Right!" Carol replied, storming off. "Two can cheat at the same game. If anybody calls . . . I'm at the library getting a book on trivia."

"Well, at least," Alice smiled, addressing herself after Carol had gone, "things are getting back to normal."

When Greg got home from school that afternoon he told Alice of the decision he had reached during the day. He was going to be mature about the matter, he said, and he was going to advise Peter and Bobby to do the same.

"Now, you're talking," Alice replied. "How are you going to do it."

"We're going to root for Carol," Greg explained. "After all, what's most important is the unity of the family. Unity means sticking together."

Alice nodded. "I know what it means. And I think you're right. That's a very mature way of looking at it."

"If Carol is determined to make our father look like a fool in front of the whole world—including everybody in the whole school—then we have a duty to support her. Any other course could cause dissension. Dissension means—"

"I know what it means," Alice assured him. "But, look, before you try to sell that idea to Peter and Bobby you better do something with the wording. I don't think they'll go for supporting Carol in making your father look like a fool in front of the whole school—including the world. Besides, Carol isn't trying to do that. That's just how it looked on television. You don't believe everything you see on TV, do you?"

Greg looked thoughtful. "No, but—"

"Do you believe in Superman? Of course not. So, there you are. It probably just *looked* like Carol was trying to make your father look like a fool. We'll probably find out some day that it was done with trick photography."

Greg was silent, pondering, for a moment. "I'll think about it," he said finally, leaving.

"If he thinks about it," Alice told herself, "I'm dead."

A short while later, Marcia came in. She was accompanied by a tall, good-looking young man, who was sharply dressed and tanned and looked like a sure winner if a Mr. Beautiful contest were ever held.

"Alice," Marcia said shyly, "this is Mr. Gorgonzolla."

"Boy, he sure is!" Alice replied admiringly. She peered up toward the peak of the young man, who was approximately six-and-one-half feet tall. "Don't move," she said. "As soon as I find the chair lift, I'll be right up."

The young man chuckled modestly.

"Mr. Gorgonzolla is my French teacher," Marcia told Alice.

"Call me 'Adam,'" the young man said.

"Uh-huh," Alice nodded knowingly. "It figures."

Marcia was glancing about. "Is Mom home?" she asked. "I brought Mr. Gorgonzolla for her."

"Gee, aren't you a little late?" Alice said. "She has Mike now, you know."

Marcia blushed. "I mean to help her with her trivia," she explained. "Mr. Gorgonzolla is an expert."

"Yes," the young man agreed. "It's something that fascinates me. I can't tell you why. It's just that when I hear some insignificant fact—the odder the better—that no one in his right mind would be interested in, I am smitten by it. I suppose that seems strange."

"I'm neutral," Alice replied. "But the other strange mind is in the recreation room, boning up. She went to the library earlier today and got all the books they had on trivia."

"Thanks, Alice," Marcia said. She motioned to Adam Gorgonzolla. "It's this way," she said, leading him toward the recreation room.

Alice stood watching them go, admiring the young man's exceptionally broad shoulders and trim waist and long legs. She noted that Marcia was walking looking up, as if mesmerized by the French teacher. She guessed that Marcia had a crush on Adam Gorgonzolla. The idea made her smile. Then it caused her to frown. And after a few more moments she tagged after Marcia and the object of her infatuation.

Approaching the recreation room, Alice saw Marcia introducing Adam Gorgonzolla to her mother. Carol was peering up at the handsome young man in the same way that Alice guessed she had stared at him herself—in delighted awe. When the introduction was completed, Marcia spoke again. Alice supposed she was explaining to her mother why she had brought the French instructor home with her. At the end of the explanation Carol replied, clearly expressing pleasure.

Increasingly curious, Alice moved closer—close enough to hear what was being said in the recreation room.

"I know what you mean," Carol was saying. "I remember my first experience. An aunt —my Aunt Helen; I remember it all as clearly as if it were only yesterday—anyway, she happened to mention the fact that the man who made the sound of the galloping horse on the April 3rd, 1929, program of the old 'Vic and Sade' radio show was the same one who caused such a commotion five days later when he put the sound of a rooster crowing into the 'Amos 'n' Andy' show that wasn't in the script. Well, I was all a tingle! It was like—like—I just can't describe it."

"I know exactly how you felt," Adam Gorgonzolla told her. "You know, however, I suppose," he added, "that your aunt's information was not quite correct."

Carol looked aghast. "No!"

"I'm afraid it was a little bit off," Gorgonzolla smiled. "It's true that the sound man—August P. B. Hasslemueller, incidentally—it's true that he put in a sound that wasn't in the script. But it wasn't a rooster crow, it was a hen cackle. Did your aunt know how it happened?"

"She didn't say," Carol replied. "But—"

"Mother—" Marcia began.

"Just a second, dear," Carol said. She addressed Adam Gorgonzolla again. "Tell me—how *did* it happen?"

"Well," Gorgonzolla smiled, "as you may or may not know, in those days of radio, the sound of a galloping horse was made by clapping halves of empty coconut shells on a board. Now, normally, August P. B. Hasslemueller left his coconut shells in the 'Vic and Sade' studio. But, after using them on the April 3rd show, he absentmindedly stuck them into his two hip pockets. And that's where they still were five days later when he was doing the 'Amos 'n' Andy' show. It just so happened, also, that Hasslemueller had brought a live chicken to the studio with him that day. He was carrying it in a big brown paper bag. Well—"

"Wasn't that a little unusual?" Carol commented.

"No. He'd found the chicken running loose on the street, and he didn't have a chicken coop with him, but he *did* have a big brown paper bag along—he was carrying his lunch in it—so, he used it. Anyway, there he was in the studio, and the program was in progress, and he started to sit down. Now, *this was unusual.* Because Hasslemueller was accustomed to standing while he worked. However, he had purchased a new pair of shoes recently, and they were not a very good fit, with the result that he was getting a corn on his left little toe."

"So he sat down," Carol nodded, fascinated.

"And, of course, when he sat down he discovered that he still had the coconut shells in his hip pockets," Gorgonzolla said. "Well, he took them out. But he didn't want to put them down because, being slightly absentminded, he was afraid he would leave them in the 'Amos 'n' Andy' studio, when they really belonged in the 'Vic and Sade' studio. Consequently, he opened the big brown paper bag and dropped the coconut shells into it and, naturally, hit the hen, which let out a loud cackle. And that's how the inadvertent cackle got on the 'Amos 'n' Andy' show."

"Do I feel dumb!" Carol said. "All these years I've thought it was a rooster crow."

"Mother—"

"Yes, dear?" Carol answered, turning to Marcia.

"Mother, besides being an expert on trivia, Mr. Gorgonzolla plays a gorgeous game of tennis, so—"

"How did you know that?" the French teacher asked.

"Oh, well, sometimes somebody will mention something at school and it will just stick in a person's mind. I know a girl who trailed you for three—uh, what I mean is, I think somebody mentioned it in passing."

"All right, dear," Carol said, "Mr. Gorgonzolla plays a gorgeous game of tennis. Yes . . . ?"

"Oh. Well, I thought he could spend a couple minutes with you—while I'm changing—and then he and I could go down to the courts. You know how desperately I need some instruction. My backhand is practically limp. So—"

"You didn't mention this to me," Gorgonzolla said.

"Oh, didn't I?" Marcia smiled. "Gee, I intended to. I guess it just sort of . . . well, you know . . . slipped my mind. But, anyway—"

"Darling, if you don't mind, I could really use Mr. Gorgonzolla here—if that's all right with him," Carol said. She faced Gorgonzolla again. "You probably have more totally insignificant information stored away in your mind than this whole stack of books," she said. "And, paging through them, I was beginning to realize what an amateur I am. Could you help me?"

"I would be delighted!" Gorgonzolla beamed.

"But, Mother—" Marcia protested.

"Darling, you want me to sparkle again next week, don't you?"

"Well, yes . . . I guess . . ."

"Good."

Marcia turned and, demoralized, walked slowly

from the room, sighing glumly with every other step.

Carol, meanwhile, had tucked her arm inside Adam Gorgonzolla's and was leading him toward a comfortable chair. "About August P. F. Hasslemueller's chicken," she said, "do you happen to know what breed it was?"

"Rhode Island Red," Adam Gorgonzolla replied. "And there's an interesting item of sub-trivia trivia connected with that. It seems—"

Alice turned to leave, having decided that she already knew considerably more than she really wanted to know about August P. F. Hasslemueller's Rhode Island Red.

5.

When Mike and Carol arrived at the television studio to participate in "Stunts & Stumpers" the next week they were still speaking to each other, but every word that passed between them was coated with a heavy covering of frost.

"Af-ter you," Mike said elaborately, bowing Carol into Jackie Jackson's small office backstage.

"Than-kwew," she responded, sailing by him.

"Hey!" Jackson said, scolding. "You two sound like you got up on the wrong side of the bread."

As one, Mike and Carol asked: "Bread?"

"Right. That's current for money. And if you two talk like that on the show—with icicles—we'll lose the audience. And if we lose the audience, we'll lose the sponsors. And if we lose the sponsors, we'll lose the money—which is current for bread."

"Sorry," Mike said.

"It was really silly," Carol said. "We'll behave from now on."

"You're supposed to be a team, you know," Jackson told them.

"Gee, that's right," Carol said, she turned to Mike. "If I lose, you lose, and if you lose, I lose," she said. "That sort of slipped my mind. I was thinking of it as kind of a competition between us. But, as Mr. Jackson says—"

"We're both on the same team," Mike nodded. "I've been aware of that all along. That's why I've been curious about what you and that French teacher have been doing together all day, while I've been at the office working."

"All day! He doesn't come to the house until after school!"

"Oh. Well, I didn't know. All I knew was that every evening when I came home, there you two were, hiding in the recreation room."

"Hiding!" Carol protested. "The doorway to the recreation room is six-feet wide, and there isn't a door on it. And we've been right there in plain sight—with Marcia swinging a tennis racket, and Bobby riding a dog, and the dog tracking the cat, and Cindy watching cartoons on television, and the other children herding buffaloes, conducting a tiger hunt on elephant-back and building a drag strip."

Jackie Jackson was staring at her open-mouthed.

"She occasionally exaggerates a bit," Mike told him. Then he addressed Carol again. "All right, I apologize," he said. "You weren't hiding. But that Gorgonzolla practically lives with us. Is that necessary?"

71

"He's helping me," Carol replied. "You want me to glitter, don't you? You don't want me to look like a dumbhead like some—uh, what I mean is, we want to win, don't we?"

"You know, I've been thinking it over," Mike replied, "and I think that if we scrimp a little we'll be able to survive without a free spark plug check-up."

"Aha!" Jackie Jackson said. "There—you put your finger right on it! It's the prizes."

Mike and Carol turned to him.

"Okay, now that you know you can stop arguing, keep it up until after the show—not arguing," he said to them. He motioned to a pair of chairs in front of his desk. "Sit down—we got a couple of minutes—and I'll tell you what I mean by that—about putting your finger on it, the prizes," he said.

As Mike and Carol settled in the chairs, Jackson sat down in the swivel chair behind the desk and leaned back. "You probably don't remember the good old days," he said. "But there was a time, you know, in the history of this country, when quiz shows were the biggest thing on TV. Today, it's looked back on fondly as 'The Golden Age.'"

"By whom?" Mike asked.

"By me," Jackson replied. "And, believe me, there was really plenty of it around."

"Of what?" Carol asked.

"Gold. That's what I mean when I say 'The Golden Age.'" He leaned forward. "Do you realize that it got to the point where we were giving away over a hundred thousand dollars for answering one question? Now, *that* is what I call patriotism."

Mike and Carol looked at each other. Then they faced back to Jackie Jackson. "I'm not sure I get the connection," Mike said.

"Patriotism. Love of country—right? Boy, did I love this country. I had one of those big quiz shows. I was a star. I was rolling in dough. There wasn't any place in the world I loved more than this country. Patriotism—right?"

"Well, I—"

"TV quiz shows replaced baseball as the great American pasttime," Jackson said, recalling, smiling. "Every show would open with the playing of the Star-Spangled Banner and the Pledge of Allegiance. And each new season, the President would throw out the first question." He fell silent and a moistness suddenly appeared in his eyes. "But it's all over. We can't get the viewing audience any more." He pointed at Mike. "And you put your finger right on it—the prizes," he said. "Somehow, a year's supply of pipe cleaners just doesn't stir up the same interest that sixty-four or a hundred thousand dollars did."

"Yes, well, I think people feel a little self-conscious about being openly patriotic these days," Mike said.

"That probably explains it. I remember—"

The door opened and an usher appeared and informed Jackson that the show was due to begin in only five minutes. Jackson and Mike and Carol rose and left the office and walked toward the

73

stage. They could hear stomping, yelling and whistling. A comic apparently was getting the audience into the proper mood.

"I have a dream," Jackson said mistily. "I call it 'The Big Comeback!' The whole country becomes quiz-show crazy again. The prizes skyrocket—a hundred thousand, two hundred thousand, five hundred thousand—a million dollars riding on one question! And me—I'm the m.c. of the biggest quiz show of 'em all!"

"Sounds nice," Carol smiled.

Jackson nodded, looking suddenly starry-eyed. "Call me a superpatriot, but I think this country can do it again," he said. "I think America can become One Big Quiz Show!"

The studio orchestra struck up the "Stunts & Stumpers" theme.

"They're playing my song," Jackson told Mike and Carol. Then he went dashing out onto the stage, all seventy million teeth flashing.

"You know . . . about the future . . . he could be right," Mike said, all at once looking terribly ill.

"Shhhh—we're almost on," Carol replied.

Jackie Jackson was telling his opening joke. At the same time, Mike was putting on a pair of dark glasses.

"What's that for?" Carol asked, perplexed. "Are you afraid you'll be recognized—after last time."

"This is to prevent what happened last time from happening again," Mike explained. "I figured out what caused my stage fright. Remember, I told you that once you're on stage and the lights are in your eyes, you can't see a thing—the audience doesn't exist?"

"Yes, and—"

"I know—I was wrong. I got out there and saw all those eyes staring at me and—well, what happened is history. But it won't happen again. In these dark glasses, I really can't see a thing, lights or no lights. They're practically opaque."

"Oh. But do you—"

"Hold it!" Mike interrupted. He pointed toward the stage. "Here comes our cue—"

"—our contestants from last week," Jackie Jackson was announcing. "Let's have a big hand for—Mr. and Mrs. Brady!"

Instantly transformed into a personality, Carol went skipping out onto the stage, waving gaily to the audience, throwing occasional kisses. The audience went wild. The applause was deafening. And as the cacophony rolled on, Mike sauntered out casually and joined Carol and Jackson in front of the cameras. He appeared to be the model wit and scholar.

"Well, here we are again," Jackson said jovially when the applause had finally died down. "Mr. Brady, I see you're wearing dark glasses tonight. I hope being on TV hasn't gone to your head."

"On the contrary," Mike replied dryly, "the fact that I'm wearing dark glasses would indicate that it's gone to my eyes."

Thunderous laughter rocked the studio.

"*Very* good!" Jackson said admiringly. He

turned to Carol. "And, Mrs. Brady, has being on TV changed your life in any way?"

"How perceptive of you to guess!" Carol responded. "Yes, as a matter of fact, it has." She stepped closer to the camera. "Jackie—" she began.

"I'm back here," he told her, speaking from behind her.

"Being on your show has changed my life completely," Carol went on, ignoring his aggrieved comment. "Before, I was just, well, a plain, everyday housewife. But, suddenly, I feel that the whole world *cares* about me. I know, for instance, that the insurance companies do. Twelve insurance agents have come to the house, all wanting to insure me for a hundred thousand dollars apiece. Isn't that *sweet!* And a hundred vacuum cleaner salesmen have wanted to make my life easier by selling me a hundred vacuum cleaners. And—"

Jackie Jackson was dragging her back into line beside him. "Wonderful, wonderful, wonderful, Mrs. Brady," he told her. "But, we have a show—"

"These dark glasses, I assume, are imported from Ireland," Mike said, offhandedly.

"Pardon, Mr. Brady?"

"I said that I assume that these dark glasses are imported from Ireland. They must be— they're O'Paque."

Jackson peered at him blankly. "I don't get it."

"I hardly expected that you would," Mike said

76

disdainfully. "You'd have to be a scholar in addition to a wit to understand."

"Oh. Well, anyway, Mr. and Mrs. Brady, it's time to play Stunts & Stumpers. However, since you've already completed the stunt, we'll go right to the stumpers. If I remember correctly, Mr. Brady, it was your turn for a question when the program ended. So, we'll pick up right where we left off—okay?"

Mike gestured disinterestedly. "Proceed, sir."

"Fine, thanks. Now, Mr. Brady, your category is Ancient Greek Literature. Do you—"

"His minor in college," Carol said.

"Wonderful. Now—"

"Oh, those good old college days," Carol went on, smiling nostalgically into the camera. "I remember I wasn't the most brilliant coed at the university, but I *did* have fun! And, after all," she went on, moving toward the camera again, "when all is said and done, isn't that really what's most important? When a body gets old and gray, what good are memories of trigonometry and Latin verbs and all those frogs we dissected? What a girl really wants to recall—the recollections that warm her heart—are those golden hours in the back booth at the malt shoppe, those magic moments, touched by stardust, she spent with her best beau at kissing rock, those—"

"Mrs. Brady!" Jackson pleaded. "Please—"

But the studio was rocked by an explosion of applause. And Jackson had to stand back while Carol took a dozen bows. When the applause finally began to diminish, she graciously moved back into line beside Jackson. Jackson sighed. Then there was an instant of total silence.

It ended as Mike spoke. "Sentimentality breeds contretemps," he said.

Once more, applause broke out. There was whistling and stomping. Three little old ladies went out on stretchers.

Then, eventually, silence again.

"I don't get it," Jackson said to Mike.

"Apparently you're not a semantics scholar," Mike replied.

Jackson shook his head.

"That explains it," Mike smirked.

Pandemonium again.

By the time Jackie Jackson had managed to get control of the audience he had the look of a half-broken man. His eyes were glassy, his skin had yellowed, and his teeth had tarnished.

"Could we go on with the questions . . . please . . . pretty please?" Jackson begged. "Mr. Brady, your category is Ancient Greek Literature . . . and your first question, for a free spark plug check-up at Al's Service Station and 24-hour Garage & Snackery, is this: I will read you a sentence that will tell us all something about ancient Greek poetry. That is, it will tell us something in the event that you're able to fill in the blanks for us. Get that? I'll read you a sentence with some blanks. And your job is to tell us what goes in the blanks. Or, to explain—"

"I *believe* I understand," Mike said.

"Oh. Okay. Actually, I was reading it again

78

for my own benefit. I didn't quite get—well, anyway—now, Mr. Brady, here's the sentence, with the blanks: The Dorian lyric for choral performance was developed by blank and blank and blank and came to fruition with blank and blank and the blankety blank."

"Ah-ah," Mike chided, "this is a family show —no blankety-blanks."

Laughter filled the studio nearly to bursting.

"Okay, you going to answer it or not?" Jackie Jackson said belligerently when the mirth had subsided.

"Of course. It's really one of the more elementary queries, you know," Mike said. "I expected something a little more challenging. But . . . so be it. The statement should read: The Dorian lyric for choral performance was developed by Alcman, Ibycus and Stesichorus and came to fruition with Pindar, Simonides and the lesser Bacchylides." He raised his dark glasses long enough to wink to the audience. "It was the lesser Bacchylides who was the blankety-blank," he said.

The walls, the ceiling, the very foundation of the building trembled as the laughter shook the studio once more.

"Yeah, that's right," Jackie Jackson said mournfully to Mike when the sound had died out again. "Who were all those guys you just named, anyway?"

"Greek poets."

"How about that!" Jackson shook his head in wonder. "Live and learn. This is like educational

TV." He turned to Carol. "Are you ready now, Mrs. Brady, to match your husband in intellectual know-how?" he asked.

Carol started to step closer to the camera.

"Don't answer that question," Jackson said quickly, pulling her back. "Just answer the questions. Now, your category is Trivia, and here's your question: In the year 1929—"

"August P. B. Hasslemueller," Carol broke in, "and it happened because he was carrying his coconuts in his hip pockets and his hen in a big brown paper bag."

Jackson stared at her for a second, stunned. Then, nodding, he said, "That's right. How did—"

He was drowned out, of course, by the roar of applause—and then upstaged as Carol stepped forward and began throwing kisses again in response to the whistling, cheering and stomping.

"You might be interested in a little story that goes along with that answer," Carol said to the audience, smiling misty-eyed into the camera, as the clamor subsided. "It's a very, very personal story, and I wouldn't normally tell it to anyone. But I feel so close, so very, very close, to all you millions of viewers out there in televisionland that I want to share it with you. Just one week ago tomorrow, I was sitting alone in the modest recreation room of our modest little cottage, when all of a sudden—"

"Mrs. Brady," Jackson interrupted, tugging at her sleeve. "If we could get on with the program—"

"—my lovely school-age daughter came bouncing into the room, all aglow," Carol went on. "And who did she have with her but a charming young man—"

"Mother!" Marcia shrieked, jumping up from the couch in front of the television set. "Don't tell that! Don't name names! Don't tell them about Mr. Gorgonzolla! I'll be the laughingstock of—"

"It's okay," Alice told her. "He's got a head-lock on your mother and he's dragging her away from the camera."

"Quiet!" Greg said. "Here comes another question for Dad!"

As Alice and the six children watched, Jackie Jackson asked Mike the second question in the Ancient Greek Literature category. Mike yawned, flickered an invisible speck from his jacket sleeve, and then rattled off the names of seven minor Greek tragedians. The children jumped up and down, cheering and clapping.

"Was that even?" Greg asked Alice. "Did we all jump up and down and clap the same amount?"

"Even," Alice replied.

"I don't know," Greg said. "This idea of all of us giving both Mike and Carol the same amount of applause sounds like a good idea on paper, but in actual practice—well, when Carol answered her question, Cindy did a lot more clapping than she did just now when Dad answered his."

"I wath younger then and had more childith enthuthiathm," Cindy explained.

"Younger! By three minutes? That's not enough to make any difference!"

"It's the spirit that counts," Alice said to Greg. "Cindy intended to clap just as hard for Mike as she did for her mother. Don't quibble—just watch."

As the show progressed, Mike and Carol answered question after question successfully. Mike dropped a number of offhand comments that were both scholarly and witty, breaking up the audience. And Carol got in several little anecdotes about family life that had the people in the audience chuckling delightedly once, weeping sentimentally the next time, and then finally sobbing hysterically.

Jackie Jackson was saved by the horn.

"Gee, I'm sorry," he said to Mike and Carol, overcome by joy, "but our time is up. Listen, what do you say? Will you be able to come back next week?" He was shaking his head hopefully.

"That would be wond-der-fullll!" Carol gushed.

"Unless we can think of something interesting to do—like *anything* else," Mike replied dryly.

"Okay, they'll be back, folks!" Jackson informed the audience.

The usual pandemonium followed. As the sound of cheers, stomps and whistles shook the studio, Carol stepped toward the camera, her eyes misty once more. "I want to thank my director . . . my cameraman . . . and all the little people . . . the scrub lady . . . the scrub lady's assistant, who pours the wash powder into her bucket of water . . . the assistant's assistant, who fills the bucket with water in the first place . . . the—"

Alice switched off the picture.

"Don't turn it off," Marcia said. "Switch over to the channel where they're having the Emmy awards. Mom'll be getting the one for best supporting actress."

"Mrs. Brady, please," Jackie Jackson pleaded, striding along the corridor toward his office, with Mike on one side of him and Carol on the other, "next week, remember—*I'm* the star of the show. The people tune in to see *me!* Take away Jackie Jackson, and what have you got? Just another weed in the vast wasteland! But, tonight, I got on-camera for a total of about seven minutes—and that's stretching it. So, next week—"

"Mr. Jackson, there isn't going to be a next week," Mike informed him.

Jackie Jackson halted, causing Mike and Carol to stop. "No kidding?" he said. "You know something I don't know? You got some inside info on doomsday?"

"What? Oh. No, I don't mean there isn't going to be a next week. I mean, simply, that we won't be on the show next week."

"Oh . . . that's too bad," Jackson replied,

grinning. "Well, I guess we'll just have to putt-putt-putt along without you. It won't be easy, but—"

"Mike, I heard what you said, that we simply won't be on the show next week, but what did you mean by it?" asked Carol.

"How could anything be any clearer than that?" Mike asked. "We're through, finished. We both wasted a lot of time last week preparing for this show. I did it, frankly, because I wanted to redeem myself. The first time, I looked foolish. This time . . . well, at least I didn't look as foolish as I did the last time. So, I'm even. And that's the best time to quit."

Carol addressed Jackie Jackson. "We can't quit, can we?" she said. "We promised to come back. And we did it on the air. That makes it legal. A legal obligation."

"Well, maybe something can be worked out," Jackson said hopefully, moving on.

"I didn't promise to come back next week," Mike told Carol, as they followed Jackson.

"But I did. And I was speaking for both of us. Don't forget—community property laws. What I promise, you promise."

"That has nothing to do with—"

Jackie Jackson had entered his office and tried to close the door behind him.

"It's a moral obligation, then," Carol said, shoving the door open and following Jackson into the room. The phone was ringing. "Maybe that's for me," she said, heading toward the desk.

"Will you hold it!" Jackson shouted. "This is

84

still my office! Maybe that's *your* studio out there . . . and *your* cameras . . . and your audience . . . but this is still *my* office and *my* telephone!"

"I'm sorry," Carol apologized. "It was a natural reaction. The phone rang and—"

Jackson had picked up the receiver. "Yeah?" he said into the mouthpiece. "Jackie Jackson here . . . what—" He interrupted himself, stared sourly at the phone a moment, then handed it toward Carol. "It's for you," he said.

"For *me!*" she squealed.

"One of your fans," Jackson replied glumly.

Carol took the phone and introduced herself, then began accepting the compliments the fan had for her.

"You made a wise decision, deciding to back out of the show," Jackie Jackson told Mike. "A thing like this, adulation, can destroy a person who isn't used to it. Look what it did to me. What am I doing on a crumby show like 'Stunts & Stumpers'? Because I crave adulation, that's why. The same thing could happen to your wife. You're wise to get her as far away from the temptation as possible."

"Well, I'm not really worried about Carol," Mike said. "She has a level head—"

The director of the show, a tall, skinny, bald young man with a jumpy manner, entered the office carrying a phone on a long extension cord. "Take this line, will you, Jackie," he begged. "The whole switchboard is lit up like a Christmas tree. We can't handle all the calls. These two—"

He indicated Mike and Carol. "—they're the biggest thing since peanut butter. The calls . . . thousands . . ." He shoved the phone into Jackson's hands. "Are we going to have a rating!" he said ecstatically, hurrying out. "Yiiiii! Woweeee!"

The phone in Jackson's hands began ringing. He looked at it, then moved to the open doorway and looked down the corridor in the direction the director had gone. "Rating, eh?" he mused.

"Your phone is ringing," Mike told him.

"How could it be?" Jackson asked, glancing toward his desk. "Your wife's talking on it—oh, yeah! The phone I'm holding, you mean." He lifted the receiver. "Yeah, hello . . ." He began nodding. "No, I'm not him, but—what do you mean, you could tell I'm not him because I don't sound witty and scholarly? Listen, you bum—" He hung up. The phone began ringing again immediately. Once more, he lifted the receiver. "Yeah, okay, what?" he said gruffly. Then he suddenly beamed. "Yeah, this is me." Pause. "Oh, you did, eh? Yeah . . . yeah . . . well, no, they're not exactly *all* mine. I'll tell you how it happened. I got this dentist, see, and he's got this wife, and she had a set of matched pearls and the string broke. Well, right out of the blue, he got this idea—"

Mike moved to one of the chairs and slumped down in it, tuning out both Carol and Jackie Jackson. Calls kept coming in on both phones. He refused to take the ones that were for him. When an hour had passed, he got up and, with a shoe, secretly unplugged the cord to Carol's phone from the socket. As she rattled the phone button, trying to attract the attention of the operator, he left the office, followed the cord that was connected to Jackson's phone, located it two offices east, and disconnected it. When he got back to Jackson's office, Jackson and Carol were both rattling phone buttons. He resettled himself in the chair confident that they would soon tire of the effort.

"So many calls were coming in, it probably blew up the switchboard," Jackson said finally, putting his phone down. "But that's okay," he went on, taking Carol's phone from her and putting it down on the desk, "because we got plans to make, anyway. You two realize what can happen, don't you? This could bring back the Big Quiz Show!"

Mike looked suddenly ill again.

"Where's your patriotism!" Jackie Jackson scolded. "How would you like it if the Russians all of a sudden looked sick like that if somebody mentioned architecture!"

"What's the connection?" Mike asked.

Jackson turned to Carol. "You see it, don't you?" he asked.

"No," she replied, shaking her head, looking bewildered.

Jackson was appalled. "After all those nice things all those good Americans said to you on the phone just a minute ago, *and you don't see the connection?*"

Carol cringed a little, looking guilty. "Well, since you put it *that* way, Yes, I guess—"

"This is preposterous!" Mike said, rising. "I refuse to listen to any more of it. Carol, come on. We're leaving."

"Honey . . . they might get the switchboard fixed . . ."

"And suppose they do? Who cares?"

"But, I mean, if all those people are going to go to all that trouble to telephone the station, then . . ." She became misty-eyed. ". . . ask not what your public can do," she continued. ". . . but rather, ask what you can do for—"

"Cut!" Mike barked. "There isn't a camera within a hundred yards of here."

"Mike is right," Jackie Jackson told Carol. "Don't waste it. Save it for next week's show. I like it. No kidding—it's great! Ask not what your public can do for you, but, rather, ask what you can do for your public. Man! What a closer! We'll use it!"

"No next week," Mike reminded him.

Jackson looked devastated. "Mikey-baby!" he said, self-pity drenching his tone. "Tell me you don't mean it!"

Mike stared at him. "How can you say that?" he asked. "You told me yourself it was a wise decision."

Jackson moved in on him and slung an arm around his shoulder. "Mikey-baby," he said, becoming confidential, "the thing about me is— not that you won't get to love me for it in time—

88

but the thing about me is that I lie. Give our relationship a year, five years, ten years, and you'll forgive me for it. But that doesn't alter the terrible fact that a few minutes ago when I told you you'd made a wise decision, Mikey-baby, I admit it, I was lying to you. It was a *terrible* decision. Do you realize what could happen? Mikey-baby—"

"Forget it," Mike said, slipping out from under Jackie Jackson's encircling arm. "The decision is made—we won't be back next week."

Jackson turned to Carol. "Carol-baby—" he began.

She put up a hand, stopping him. "I'm sorry, Mr. Jackson—"

"Call me Jackie-baby—"

"—but if that's what Mike's decided, then that's it. Believe me, I *know* what you want to say to him but just can't quite find words to say. Those same words are in my own heart, bursting to cry out to him—"

"Cut! Cut! Cut! Cut! Cut!" Mike broke in.

"You're right," Jackson said to Mike, throwing up his hands. "It might mean a lot to me . . . to the show . . . to you, too . . . if you went on with the show. But . . . well, I guess there's something more important than the show. There's your family."

"You're right," Mike said. "I'm glad you see that."

"A family is like a ship," Jackson said, "it needs a strong captain at the helm. Not only strong, but smart. It takes more than brawn to sail a ship these days. It takes brains. And the same with a family. Am I right?"

"As a matter of fact, yes," Mike replied. "So—"

"A guy would look pretty silly," Jackson snickered.

"Ahhhhh . . . yes," Mike nodded. He held out a hand to Carol. "Let's go, hon . . ."

"Coming." She slipped her hand into Mike's, waved goodbye with the other to Jackie Jackson, then followed Mike to the doorway.

"Look pretty silly what?" Mike asked, halting and facing back to Jackson.

"Go on home—forget it," Jackson advised.

"You said, 'A guy would look pretty silly,'" Mike replied. "I assume you were referring in some way to me. I think I have a right to know what you're talking about."

"All I meant was, a guy would look pretty silly looking like he wasn't so scholarly and witty after all," Jackson said. "It could destroy his standing as the head of the family—or the ship, as the case might be. You're absolutely right to be scared to death of a thing like that happening. I mean, how would it look? And with your children looking on, too. Here's this guy—this brain, this head of the household—and his wife —the little woman—knows more about something not even worth knowing than he knows about ancient Greek literature. You'd never be able to hold your head up again around the house. Believe me, Mikey-boy, I sympathize with you.

I'd be scared to come back on the show, too—just the way you are. Why, just thinking about it—"

"You can 'cut,' too," Mike told him. "But, just let me tell you this: Next week is definitely the last week. I have a career to think about! I'm not cut out for this role I'm playing. I'm not a scholar. I'm not—" He suddenly interrupted himself, looking thoughtful. Then, shaking his head, he said, "No, being witty isn't enough to build a whole new career on . . ."

6.

Mike spent the next morning at the university in conference with the head of the ancient history department. When he returned to the house, he went directly to the den and shut himself in, then began making telephone calls to various parts of the country. He was calling professors who had written books on ancient Greek literature—books he had already read—asking them to send him the notes they had not incorporated in the books. Additionally, he was calling candidates for Ph.D.s who were preparing papers on various aspects of ancient Greek literature, asking them to send him copies of the works on which their theses would be based. He wanted nothing that was known on the subject to escape him. When he had finished with the calls, he summoned Alice. He ordered her to keep him in black coffee and sandwiches until he dropped. Then he resumed the study of the many volumes he had acquired from the local library.

At midnight that night, another mug of coffee and another tunafish-and-watermelon-preserves sandwich was placed before him as he sat at his desk, his eyes fixed blearily to the page of a book on ancient Greek comedy.

"Thanks, Alice," he murmured.

"You're welcome. Say, do you mind if I sit on your lap for a while?"

Mike snapped to attention and looked around. It was not Alice, but Carol, who had brought him the food and coffee. "I'm sorry, honey," he said. "I didn't know it was you. I haven't had my eyes on anything but print for something like—" He looked at his watch. "Good heavens! Eight hours!"

"I knew you were fogged in," she said. "Anybody who can eat watermelon preserves and tuna fish has to be, at the least, slightly preoccupied." She pointed back at his watch. "Mike, look again. It's after midnight. When do you knock off?"

"Just as soon as I finish this one book," he promised.

"Oh. Well, that shouldn't take so long. It's . . . uh . . . oh, yes, I see, the complete works of Greek comedy . . . gee, it's so thin."

Mike nodded. "The Greeks have a great sense of tragedy," he said, "but when it comes to humor—just give me a couple more minutes, honey."

Five minutes later, he clapped the book closed.

"Done?"

"Done."

"Completely?"

"Well . . . until tomorrow morning," Mike replied, rising from his seat at the desk. "I figure it will take me a couple more days to get letter-perfect on all the facts in all these books. By then, the first copies of some notes and papers and theses I've ordered ought to start coming in and—"

"Mike! You're out of your mind!"

"Carol, you know, I'm the one who wanted to call a halt to this thing last night," he said. "You're the one who wanted to go on. So, I agreed. And that's why all this study is necessary. What Jackie Jackson said was true. I'm the head of the family . . . the captain of the ship. I've got to show the crew that I'm capable. I've got to keep up their confidence in me."

"Oh, yes, I can see that," Carol nodded. "And if that's your reason for doing this, dear, then I think you're right to do it. You don't want to look like—as Peter put it—a dumbhead again."

"I'm glad you agree," Mike said.

"Oh, I do. And I have confidence in you, too, darling," Carol said. "I'm sure it won't be you who misses the first question. If anybody ends up looking like a dumbhead, it'll be—" Carol broke in on herself, then remained silent for a moment, rolling her eyes ceilingward, looking thoughtful.

Mike was smiling, nodding.

"—it'll be me," Carol said finally.

"Them's the breaks," Mike said. He switched off the desk lamp. "Shall we go?" He led the way from the room.

"Mike . . . I know how important it is for a father to be a symbol of strength and wisdom . . ." Carol said, following him. "But it's important for a mother to be a symbol, too, you know."

"Of course," Mike replied, as they walked toward the master bedroom.

"A good symbol, I mean," Carol said. "Not a symbol of a dumbhead."

Mike laughed. "Darling, I'm sure the children expect you to miss one of those trivia questions soon, anyway. Nobody with good sense would stuff his—or her—head with all that drivel, and then deliberately recall it in front of millions of television viewers."

"Darling," Carol said, controlling a rising irritation, "I don't sit around stuffing my head with it. I hear things that may or may not seem important to certain other people and I remember them, that's all."

"If you haven't been stuffing your head with it while you've been locked up in the rec room with that French tennis player, what *have* you been doing?" Mike asked tightly.

Carol stomped after him as he entered the bedroom. "How could we be locked up together in a room that doesn't have a door?" she demanded. "And he's not French! He teaches French! And what do you mean, drivel? Just what makes Homer's epic poems any more important than August P. B. Hasslemueller's cackle!"

"What!" Mike exploded. "Are you serious?"

"You bet your boots, I'm serious!" Carol told him. She grabbed a pillow from the bed. "I'm serious about sleeping in the recreation room tonight, and I'm serious about calling in my coach tomorrow and getting back into training." She stormed from the room.

"You're being childish!" Mike called after her from the bedroom doorway.

"Tonight, childish I may be," she called back to him, continuing on her way to the recreation room. "But when this confrontation is over, the dumbhead in the family I *won't* be!"

Furious, Mike got in the last word. "August P. B. Hasslemueller sits on coconut shells!" he bellowed.

When Mike arrived at the breakfast table the next morning, he found, in addition to Carol and the six children, a guest: Jackie Jackson. "I'm sorry for anything rude or unfair that I might have said last night," he said to Carol. "Good morning, children," he said to the children. "Don't you have a breakfast table of your own to go to?" he said to Jackie Jackson.

"You're forgiven," Carol replied, smiling. "And I apologize, too. It was as much my fault as yours."

The children, from the oldest to the youngest, responded with a "Good morning" and a smile for him.

"Pass the sugar," Jackie Jackson said.

"What's he doing here?" Mike asked Carol, sitting down at the table. "Is this another stunt for

'Stunts & Stumpers'? What do I have to do, throw him out of the house?"

"Hey—you're even witty off-camera!" Jackie Jackson said, impressed. "You know what you two ought to have," he said to Mike and Carol, "you ought to have a Mr. & Mrs. show. Ever see any of those programs? The husband and the wife sit around the breakfast table and make chit-chat. And in between eating they read commercials. You two would be great at that."

"Would we be on the thow, too?" Cindy asked.

"Could be," Jackson replied. "You'd have to audition for it, though. Sort of take a test, I mean —to show that you're a personality. Most of the time, people's real kids are no good for show business. So they hire actors to play the people's kids."

"But this would be the real thing—Mike and I in the flesh, and—"

"Not in the flesh, dear," Mike said. "Jackie is talking about television. You must be thinking of the movies."

"When I said 'in the flesh,' I didn't mean 'in the flesh,'" Carol replied. She addressed Jackson again. "How could actors play the parts of our real children better than our real children?" she asked.

"They're more experienced."

"*At being our real children?*"

"What I mean is, they can ham it up."

"But our real children don't ham it up."

"Right, and that's why, more than likely, they couldn't play themselves on TV. The people watching the show know that kids of personalities are always hamming it up. But, listen, I didn't come here to talk about a program that's still in the talking stage. What I—"

"Hold it!" Mike said. "What program? What talking stage?"

"He didn't mean that actually, Mike," Carol said.

"I meant I was talking about it," Jackie Jackson said. "And I'll take it all back if you'll let me tell you what I came here to tell you. I've got big news about 'Stunts & Stumpers.' Remember what I told you? I told you that with a little luck, the three of us—the hottest m.c. in TV, and two of the sweetest little personalities to come along the pike since it took its last peak—could bring back big time TV quiz shows. Well, it's happening. They're lining up."

"Who?" Carol asked.

"The guys who give away the big prizes. They're lining up to give away their prizes on our show. It happened overnight."

"What kind of prizes?" Mike asked.

"Would you believe a Jaguar?"

Mike whistled, impressed.

"Don't go overboard," Jackson said. "I didn't tell you we've got a Jaguar. I just used that as an example."

"What *do* we have?"

"Free sky-diving lessons."

Mike stared at him for a moment; then, having lost interest, began pouring himself a mug of coffee.

"It's better than pipe cleaners," Jackson said.

"I suppose so," Mike replied. "I simply fail to see the relationship between a Jaguar and sky-diving lessons."

"I told you—the Jaguar was an example, it wasn't supposed to be related. And we've got a motor scooter, too, and a lot of electric appliances."

"What appliances?" Carol asked.

"Oh . . . about a dozen."

"But which ones?"

"If you're going to pin me down, what it really is is a dozen surplus electric fire-starters," Jackson replied. "But it's not the details that are important. What's important is that you two are a big hit. And we could all ride this wave of popularity right to the top. I got the idea when you left me the other night, though, that you didn't really understand that."

"Mr. Jackson, I think that's a lot of wishful thinking on your part," Mike said. "You want big time TV quiz shows to make a comeback, so you—"

"No, no, no, no, no," Jackson broke in. "Mikey-baby, I'm a hard-headed realist, not a dreamer. When I tell you—"

Alice entered the kitchen.

"Oh, is this another one of the kids?" Jackson said. "I thought you only had six."

"No, this is Alice," Carol said. "Alice," she went on, "this is Jackie Jackson. He—"

"I know who he is," Alice nodded. "Although . . . are you sure you're you?" she asked Jackson. "You don't quite look the same in person as you do on television. I think it's . . . uh, your, uh . . ."

"It's because there aren't any bright lights in here shining on them," Jackson explained. "Pearls need a lot of light to glitter like that."

"Oh." Alice held up a notepad and addressed Mike and Carol. "I'm sorry I didn't get breakfast," she said. "I was working on your schedules." She turned back to Jackson. "I'm their appointments secretary," she explained.

"You're our what?" Mike asked.

"That's my idea, dear," Carol told him. "We keep getting calls, people wanting us for interviews and personal appearances. And, since Alice is usually the one who answers the phone anyway, I thought she might as well double as our appointments secretary."

Mike shrugged. "Why not? What's my schedule for the day, Alice?" he asked.

"Well," she replied, consulting the notepad, "the reporter from the *Post* will be here at ten for an interview, and then—"

"The *Post!*" Mike said, showing interest. "The *Saturday Evening Post*? I thought something happened to it."

"This is the local *Post*," Alice told him. "It's that thing they throw on the porch every Wednesday. It's full of grocery ads."

"And they want to interview me?" Mike said doubtfully. "Where will they put it, between the pot roast and the extra-large white eggs? Scratch it," he told Alice. "And all the rest of the interviews. I'll be too busy."

"That's where you're making your mistake," Jackie Jackson said. "It's what I was afraid of. You don't see the potential. You ought to do that interview, Mikey-baby. You know what I once said? I said: I don't care what they say about me in the papers as long as they print my name right."

"*You* said that?" Mike challenged.

"Well . . . I guess a lot of other guys said it before me. But I said it most recently. And, do you know what it means. It means, any publicity you can get, take it."

Mike addressed Alice. "Tell the *Post* it can have Jackie Jackson between the pot roast and the extra-large white eggs," he said.

"I'll be glad to," Jackson said to Alice. Then, to Mike, he said, "Because I happen to know which side my bread is buttered on. Publicity, that's which side. The more people who read and hear about you, the more people who'll tune in to see you on the show. And the bigger the rating, the bigger the prizes we can line up."

Mike was rising. "Alice, I'll have my breakfast in the den," he said. "I want to get back to my books."

"Will you listen to me?" Jackson pleaded.

"You listen to me for a second," Mike replied. "If I don't get in there and study, I won't know everything there is to know about ancient Greek literature. And if I don't know everything there is to know about ancient Greek literature, I might miss the next question. And if I miss the next question, it won't make any difference to me how great the prizes are on the show, because *I* won't be on the show. Right?"

"Get the publicity first and worry about answering the questions later, that's my motto," Jackson replied.

Mike turned and headed for the doorway.

"You'll always be a year's-supply-of-pipe-cleaners winner," Jackson called after him. "You're just not Big Time, Mikey-baby . . . you're just not Big Time!"

Mike was gone.

"Alice," Carol said, "let's go over that appointments schedule. Maybe I can work Mike's interview into *my* schedule."

Jackie Jackson beamed. "Now *that*," he said, indicating Carol, addressing the children, "is a Big Time Personality."

The children stared at Carol in horror.

A mail, truck arrived at the Brady house around midmorning. It had a load of large manila envelopes for Mike: the first shipment of theses and papers and collections of notes from the scholars he had contacted. After the envelopes had been dumped onto his desk, Mike closed the den door, then locked it. He was seen no more the rest of the day. Not even Alice's attempts to deliver sandwiches and coffee could get him to unlock the door.

Although Mike had as much as disappeared, Carol was clearly in evidence around the house, however. She spent most of the morning with the reporter from the *Post*. Tailoring the interview to the reporter's special interest, she recited all the trivia she could recall that was in any way related to groceries. She told him, for instance, about the years and years of laboratory experimentation that had eventually led to the development of the sweet potato vine. It seemed that the scientists, after admitting to complete failure in the attempt to get the sweet potato to sprout, finally threw it out a window and went on to other things. As it happened, the sweet potato landed in a crack in a sidewalk. Vines began growing from it immediately. And from this experience came the scientific discovery that while nothing will ever grow in the laboratory or the fertilized field or yard, anything and everything will grow in the cracks in the sidewalk. The reporter was fascinated by the story. He doubted that it would appear in the paper, though. The grocery stores that were advertising sweet potatoes that week would probably get the publisher to kill it, he thought.

Shortly after lunch, a second mail truck arrived. It was delivering several sacks of fan letters for Mike and Carol that had gone first to the television station and that the television station had forwarded. Carol began reading them immediately. There were hundreds of them. When she finished, along toward late afternoon, she was so moved by the sentiments expressed by the writers that she vowed that she would answer every one of them personally.

"That's a lot of writing," Alice warned. "It would take you six months, full-time, to answer all those letters."

"You're right," Carol decided. "I guess you better do it for me, Alice. But sign *my* name. Unless the letters are to Mike. In that case, sign *his* name. We wouldn't want our fans to think we weren't interested enough in them to answer their letters personally."

"If I do your letter-writing, then you'll have to do my work," Alice pointed out.

"Oh, yes . . . there's that, isn't there. Well . . . do something else with the letters, then," Carol said, breezing out of the room.

"Suppose I—"

"Don't tell me about it," Carol begged. "I'd feel guilty if I knew what it was."

When Carol was out of sight, Alice stuffed the letters into big brown paper bags and then stored them where the trash man was sure to see them and mistake them for stuff that had been put out to be hauled away.

Carol had asked Marcia when she was getting ready to go to school that morning to bring Adam Gorgonzolla home with her when she returned; if, that is, he were willing to resume coaching her. When Marcia arrived a short while later, the French teacher was with her. Carol snatched him away immediately, taking him into the recreation room, and they picked up where they had left off. The trivia flew, fast and furious.

Marcia stood in the recreation room doorway for a few minutes, listening to her mother and

Adam Gorgonzolla play verbal Ping-pong with bits and pieces of absolutely useless information. Then, disgusted, she left and went to her room. She was pouting, lying across her bed, a short while later, when Cindy and Jan arrived.

"We're orphanth," Cindy announced.

"Who told you that?" Marcia asked.

"Jan."

"I didn't say we are, I said we might as well be," Jan explained to Marcia. "Mother's so busy talking, nobody can talk to her. And Mike is locked in the den."

"If you want to talk to Mother, you ought to see her appointments secretary and make an appointment with her," Marcia said, glowering.

"If you mean Alice, that wouldn't help, either," Jan said. "Alice says she has to make an appointment with Mom herself—just to tell her about her other appointments."

"We ought to run away," Cindy said.

"Running away is no solution to anything," Marcia said. "Anyway, it isn't 'in' these days. The thing for us to do is stay and express our dissent."

"What'th our diththent?" Cindy asked, her eyes widening.

"What I mean is, we ought to show Mom exactly how we feel about the way she's monopolizing Adam Gor—uh, what I mean is, I think we ought to show her exactly how we feel about the way she's making us feel like orphans."

"You mean *picket* her?" Jan said, already leery of the idea.

"Well . . ."

"She meanth burn the houth down," Cindy explained to Jan.

"No—nothing like that!" Marcia said. "But, what we could do, we could withdraw our support. She might get the message if we did that."

"Like how?" Jan asked.

"Well, we're all supposed to be neutral about this quiz show," Marcia said. "We agreed on it, remember? We said we'd root just as hard for Mike when he was answering a question as we rooted for Mom when she was answering a question. And that's what we've done. But—"

Cindy was shaking her head.

"What's that for?" Marcia asked.

"I cheated the latht time," Cindy told her. "I went 'yea, yea, yea, yea!' for Mom, and only 'yea, yea, yea!' for Mike. I didn't mean to, though. I lotht count."

"All right, but that was last time," Marcia said. "I'm talking about *next* time. Next time, when Mike is answering his question, we'll cheer and yell and wave things or something, and then when Mom is answering *her* question, we'll be absolutely still."

"Mom'd *kill* us!" Jan said.

"Oh, she would not," Marcia replied. "She'd just notice that we weren't supporting her any more and she'd wonder why and she'd ask us and we'd tell her."

"Because she stole your boyfriend?" Jan asked.

"No! That has nothing to do with it. And, he's

not my boyfriend. He's my French teacher. How could I be interested in him—he's practically an old man. I only brought him home so he could help Mom with her trivia."

"Then why are you mad becauth he'th helping her with her trivia?" Cindy asked.

"I'm not even going to discuss that part of it," Marcia told Jan and Cindy. "The only question is, are we going to withdraw our support or not? I vote in favor. Because that's the only way we'll ever get Mom off that quiz show."

Cindy raised a hand. "I'm for that," she said.

Jan looked thoughtful. "I understand what we're going to do," she said. "We're going to jump up and down and cheer for Mike, but not for Mom. But, what I don't get is, if Mom's at the TV studio, how will she know whether we're jumping up and down and cheering or not?"

Marcia looked stunned. "I didn't think about that."

"Maybe we could get Alice to snitch on us to Mom," Jan suggested.

Marcia shook her head. "She wouldn't do that."

"I'll bet Bobby would snitch on us," Jan said.

"Of course!" Marcia agreed. "He'd like that."

"But," Jan said, "do we really want to jump up and down and cheer for a man who has a son who'd snitch on us? And, another thing, how is Mom going to feel when she finds out we were jumping up and down and cheering for Mike, but not for her?"

"Thunk," Cindy said.

"Sunk?"

"That'th how I'd feel," Cindy explained.

"Well, she sure wouldn't feel very good about it," Jan said.

"Of course not," Marcia said. "That's the whole point. It's *supposed* to make her feel—mmm-mmmm, yes, I see what you mean. I'd hate to do anything that would make her feel sunk. Tell you what. We'll withdraw our support, but we just won't tell her about it. That way, we won't hurt her feelings."

"We'll still have to keep jumping up and down and cheering for her, then," Jan said, "if we don't want her to find out we're not doing it anymore."

"Poor Bobby," Cindy said. "Now he won't get to thnitch on uth. He'd thure be dithappointed if he knew."

In the boys' room, Greg was announcing to Peter and Bobby that something had to be done about their father. He explained why: "He's down in the den," he said, "and when I knocked he wouldn't let me in."

"Why did you want in?" Bobby asked.

"To find out what he was doing in there with the door locked," Greg answered.

"Wouldn't he tell you?"

"He told me. He's studying for the quiz show. But he told me *through the locked door.*"

"He won't even let Alice in," Peter told Greg.

"But I'm his oldest son!"

Being respectively the middle son and the youngest son, Peter and Bobby realized the im-

108

plications. They indicated that they were in agreement with Greg: something had to be done about Mike.

"Can we divorce him?" Bobby asked.

Peter slugged him with a pillow.

"We don't have to go that far," Greg said. "Dad's always been reasonable. All we have to do, I think, is give him some little sign that we're not very happy with the way things are going."

"Like what?" Peter asked.

"We'll stop speaking to him altogether," Greg replied.

Peter shook his head. "It ought to be something he'll notice," he said. "How will he know we're not speaking to him if he's locked up in the den?"

"He'll come out *some*day," Greg told him. "And when he does, there we'll be, all lined up, not speaking to him. How could he miss a thing like that? Who's in favor?"

No hands were raised.

"I'd do it, but I've got a bad back," Bobby said.

"What does *that* have to do with it?"

"I don't know," he replied. "But when Alice doesn't want to do something, she says she can't on account of her bad back. So, if it's a good reason for her, it's a good reason for me, isn't it?"

"Well . . . if you don't want to do it, I suppose it's as good a reason as any," Greg admitted.

"The thing is," Peter said to Greg, "I'm a little afraid of what it might do to Dad if we stopped speaking to him. It could drive him to drink. Or make him bitter. That's always happening to guys on TV. Somebody does something to them, and they get bitter."

"What's bitter?" Bobby asked.

"It means he dies in the end," Peter explained. "In the beginning of the show they always tell this guy he's bitter, and then he dies in the end."

Bobby shivered. "Let's stay away from that," he said.

"I guess it wasn't such a good idea," Greg said. "I take it back. When you stop and think about it, up until now, Dad's been a pretty good guy. If he wants to lock himself in the den and study for a dumb quiz show, then I guess we ought to go along with it."

Peter raised a hand. "I vote for that."

"Me, too," Bobby said. "Anyway, I don't think we've got anything to worry about. If we just wait a couple days, he'll probably grow out of it."

In the recreation room, with items of trivia bursting all about them, Tiger and Fluffy responded to the problems created by Mike and Carol in the only sensible way: they slept contentedly on.

7.

As Mike and Carol approached the "Stunts &
Stumpers" theater the next week, they saw a
small crowd around the entrance. It seemed to
be made up entirely of little old ladies.

"Do you suppose they carried them all out on
stretchers before the program even began?"
Mike said, puzzled.

Carol shook her head. "I don't think Jackie
Jackson would let anybody go who was still con-
scious. Maybe they were carried out on stretchers from an earlier program."

"Then why are they still here?"

"Waiting to get in to Stunts & Stumpers, I
guess," Carol replied. "That must be their 'thing'
—they get carried out on stretchers, program
after program, day in and day out, week after
week, month upon month, year after—Mike
. . . what are they doing? They look like
they're attacking!"

The little old ladies, having sighted Mike and
Carol, were galloping toward them, waving pen-

cils and pens and slips of paper and autograph books. Although there were probably no more than a dozen of them, they resembled and sounded a great deal like a thundering herd of buffalo.

Carol huddled against Mike, cowering in terror. "Mike! We'll be trampled!"

Mike held her close to protect her. "It must be a mistake!" he told her. "Keep that in mind! We're nobody! It must be a mistake! When they find out it's a mistake, they'll go away!"

But instead of trampling them underfoot, the little old ladies surrounded them, shoving the pencils and pens and slips of paper and autograph books at them, demanding that they sign.

"We're nobody!" Mike insisted, meanwhile scribbling his name in an autograph book.

"Darling, let's not be hasty," Carol said, signing a slip of paper, "maybe we *are* somebody! After all, these ladies have had more experience at this than we have. Maybe they know something we don't know."

"Sorry, lady," Mike said to one of the little old women, handing her back a blank check she had given him to sign.

It had appeared at first that Mike and Carol would be able to accommodate the crowd of little old ladies within a short time and then enter the theater. But instead of diminishing, the collection of autograph-seekers grew larger. Passersby who had no interest in Mike and Carol and, in fact, weren't even sure who they were, began stopping and demanding autographs, too. The newcomers reasoned that if the little old ladies were getting Mike's and Carol's autograph, then they must be important. Consequently, as the crowd continued to swell, Mike and Carol finally had to break free and dash for the theater entrance. If they hadn't, they undoubtedly would have missed the show. Behind them, enraged, the autograph seekers started pelting the doors of the theater with pens and pencils.

"Stupendous!" Jackie Jackson told them, escorting them to his office. "I sent an usher out to stir up sentiment against you. If we're lucky, we could have a full-scale riot tonight. Can you picture the publicity! By tomorrow morning, you two could be the biggest personalities in America!"

"On the basis of starting a riot?" Mike said, appalled.

"Nah—on your charisma," Jackson replied.

"When did we get that?" Mike asked.

"You didn't yet. But if that usher can get a riot started, then, in my book, you got charisma." They had reached the door of the office, and Jackson halted them. "I got a surprise for you," he told them. "But I better warm you up for it first. Solomon I. Solaman is a little hard to take if you don't know how important he is. First off—"

"Just a minute," Mike interrupted. "This surprise—is that what it is? A Solomon I. Solaman?"

"Right. Now, first off—"

"Is it anything like a year's supply of pipe cleaners?" Carol asked.

113

"Nothing like," Jackson answered. "Now, first off—"

The house is getting a little crowded," Carol said. "What size is it? Is it bigger than a bread box?"

"It's a *him!*" Jackson told them. "Solomon I. Solaman is the king of the talent managers."

"King Solaman?" Carol said. "Mmmmmm . . . I think I've heard of him."

"Sure you've heard of him," Jackson replied. "Solomon I. Solaman is to show business what King Kong is to the Empire State Building—tops! When a talent has Solomon I. Solaman as its manager, it can't miss. Give Solomon I. Solaman your complete cooperation and a little time and he can make your name a household word!"

"I'm not sure that's so good," Carol said. "There are household words and there are household words. I mean, there's a refuse container that's named after the man who makes it, and, in a way, *his* name is a household word. But I'm not sure how delighted I'd be to hear some housewife tell me she was used to dumping her garbage into the Carol Brady. That would be a household word, sure, but—"

"Please," Jackson broke in, "whatever you do, don't let Solomon I. Solaman hear you talking like that. He'd drop you like a hot tomato. He has a quirk. First off, as I tried to tell you about an hour ago, he can't stand personalities. Because deep down inside—they're empty shells, brainless and deceitful and untrustworthy—which is a direct quote. But what he can't stand even more

114

is a personality with brains and integrity. Because, he says, you can't trust a personality like that to act like a true personality—a true personality being an empty shell, brainless, and so on and so on. Get the pitch?"

Mike and Carol shook their heads.

"It doesn't matter," Jackson told them. "Solomon I. Solaman has decided to put you in the picture—to manage you, in other words. It's the biggest break you could ever get. So, when we go in there, just don't spoil it. Just look dumb, and if you have anything to say, don't. That's all he expects of you. Okay—let's go."

Jackie Jackson went bustling into his office.

Mike and Carol looked at each other and shrugged, then tagged after him. Inside, a very large man, about the size of a weather balloon, was squeezed into one of the armchairs. Everything about him seemed round, his eyes, his nose, his mouth. He looked as if he were about to roll out of the chair and bounce out the doorway.

"Mikey-baby, Carol-baby, this is Solomon I. Solaman!" Jackson announced.

"Nice to—" Mike began, extending a hand.

A sound of alarm escaped from Solomon I. Solaman and he drew back, as if afraid of becoming contaminated.

"Mustn't touch," Jackson told Mike. "Solomon I. Solaman doesn't shake hands with personalities. He's afraid of catching corruption."

"Just a minute—" Mike said, annoyed. "I don't know who this—"

"Silence!" Solomon I. Solaman rumbled. And

the office trembled as if shaken by audience applause. "Do you want to be internationally famous?" he went on, addressing Carol and Mike. "Do you want to be adored by the masses? Of course you do! Because you are personalities! And that's what *all* personalities want!"

"But we're not and we don't," Mike told him.

Solomon I. Solaman turned to Jackson. "And they wonder why I say they're deceitful," he said sorrowfully. "Did you hear that? That out-and-out, barefaced lie? Rotten, I tell you, Jackson. Rotten to the core, every one of them. You're so fortunate that you're not a personality."

"But I *could* be," Jackson said. "If you'd just manage me, I know I could."

Solomon I. Solaman shook his large round head. "You're a talented enough m.c., but a personality, you're not," he decreed. "Your teeth are wrong."

Jackson brightened. "But they're not really mine," he said. "Actually, they belong to my dentist's wife. She used to wear them on a string around her neck. My own teeth look more like the oysters than the pearls. I could get rid—"

But Solomon I. Solaman was shaking his head again. "It's too late," he informed Jackson. "I've already decreed that you're not a personality. If I changed the decision it would be the same as admitting that I could be wrong. Sorry, Jackson, it was close, but you just don't have the stuff." He faced Mike and Carol again. "These two, however," he continued, "have 'personality' written all over them. Look at those stunned, vacant-eyed expressions—and yet, at the same time, the malicious, malevolent glint in their eyes. *True Personalities!*" He pushed himself to his feet. "Yes, I accept you as clients," he told Mike and Carol. "The thirty-four of us will go far together! There is no limit to how successful we can all be!"

"The thirty-four of us?" Mike asked.

"You two and me and my thirty-one other clients."

"Oh. Well, that's really very nice of you," Mike said. "It's probably a big compliment to be judged brainless and deceitful and untrustworthy by Solomon I. Solaman, but—"

"Please—stop fawning!" Solaman said, shuddering. Like a blimp that had escaped its mooring, he floated toward the doorway. "Enough of this disgusting display of false appreciation," he said. "I have work to do." Then he was gone.

"You passed the test!" Jackson told Mike and Carol excitedly. "Congratulations. You're on your way to the top!"

At that moment, an usher appeared in the doorway. "Five minutes 'til you're on," he said to Jackson.

"Okay," Jackson motioned. "Oh, listen, incidentally, did you get the riot going?"

The usher shook his head. "The crowd broke up," he reported. "They ran out of pens and pencils to throw."

"Bad break," Jackson said. "Let's put in a big supply of pens and pencils, in case the opportunity ever comes up again."

117

The usher nodded, departing. Then Jackie Jackson and Mike and Carol left the office and walked toward the wings.

"If you happen to see Solomon I. Solaman again, will you tell him to forget about managing us, please?" Mike said to Jackson. "I tried to tell him, but he wouldn't listen."

"Why should he?" Jackson replied. "Nobody would ever believe a thing like that from a personality. A personality will look you right square in the eye and lie to you—it's a personality trait."

"But I'm serious!" Mike insisted.

Jackson halted. "Look me straight in the eye and tell me that."

"We don't want Solomon I. Solaman to manage us," Mike said, looking him straight in the eye.

"See?" Jackson told him. "You did it. You looked me straight in the eye and lied to me right to my face. Solomon I. Solaman is certainly right about personalities." He moved on, shaking his head in dismay. "You're all alike—right out of the same mold. Fantastic!"

"But we're not personalities!" Mike protested loudly.

Jackson chuckled. "Are you kidding?"

"What proof do you have?" Carol demanded.

Jackson peered at her. "You *got* to be kidding," he said. "What do you mean, what proof? I heard it from Solomon I. Solaman. Not more than five minutes ago. You were there—you heard it. Would he say it if it weren't true? He's got a reputation to protect, you know. He's never been wrong."

"Maybe we *are* personalities," Carol said meekly to Mike.

"*You* can be a personality if you want to. But *I* refuse!" Mike replied adamantly.

"Proof on top of proof," Jackie Jackson told Carol. "All personalities are temperamental like that." Then, responding to the sound of the "Stunts & Stumpers" theme, he went bounding out onto the stage, teeth gleaming.

Mike and Carol were in top form when they got before the cameras that night. Mike was the perfect scholar and wit. And Carol could not have been better as the bubble-brained housewife with a head full of totally useless information.

"Why, yes," Carol replied to her first question, "I do know the name of the cabinetmaker who built the window seat that was used to stuff the bodies in *Arsenic and Old Lace*. But," she added, twinkling, "if you think I'm going to tell you it was built by Amos L. Wamsutter—as most people believe—you're wrong."

"Just give me the right answer," Jackie Jackson urged.

"Well, it isn't as simple as that," Carol replied. "If I gave you the right answer without explaining it, there might still be a question in the minds of a *lot* of people. The typical man on the street I imagine, really believes that the window seat was built by Amos L. Wamsutter. You'd get just oodles of letters, I'm afraid, if I answered 'Tod

Wheelsump' without going into more detail. You see, although Amos L. Wamsutter was, indeed, the proprietor and chief cabinetmaker for the Amos L. Wamsutter Cabinetmaking, General Carpentry & Discount Sawdust Sales Company—or 'ALWCGC&DSSC, as it was commonly called—he was out with a nasty cold the day the order came in for the window seat for *Arsenic and Old Lace*. Well, naturally, since the play was scheduled to open that night, the company's only employee, Tod Wheelsump, who was minding the store—so to speak—decided it would be poor public relations to ignore the order and then blame the failure to deliver on sun spots—an oft-used excuse in those days. The problem, though, was that Tod Wheelsump was not a cabinetmaker. Actually, he was ALWCGC& DSSC's popular chief sweeper, assigned to the discount sawdust sales division. In addition, however, he had a mind as sharp as a whip. So, that evening, he journeyed to the nearby graveyard and dug up the casket that had been used to bury the victims of a recent Indian massacre. And, reaching the theater with it just before curtain-up, he passed it off—in the dim light—as a window seat. Well, the rest is history, of course. *Arsenic and Old Lace* was written as a symbolic protest against the then current movement aimed at domesticating wild strawberries. But when the actors kept finding dead bodies in the window seat every time they opened it up, they had to 'adapt' the play to fit the action, and, on the spur of the moment, they turned it into a grim comedy. Later, when asked if he had made the window seat, Amos L. Wamsutter had insisted that he knew nothing about it. This was attributed to modesty, however, since everyone said that Wamsutter had so much to be modest about. Consequently, until only a few days ago, the role played by Tod Wheelsump in the saga of the wonderful window seat was unknown."

"Huh!" Jackie Jackson said, astounded. "How did they finally find out about it?"

"Tod Wheelsump left an I.O.U. in the grave he'd robbed," Carol replied.

"And they didn't find it until a few days ago?" Jackson asked incredulously.

"Unless you knew about it sooner," Carol replied accusingly.

"No, no, it's news to me," Jackson assured her. He looked at the card in his hand and seemed disappointed. Then he got a pencil from his jacket pocket and scratched out what was written on the card and wrote in something else. After returning the pencil to his pocket, he faced the audience. "That's right, ladies and gentlemen!" he shouted excitedly. "The answer is 'Tod Wheelsump!' Let's hear it for our typical homemaker!"

The audience went wild with applause.

When the studio had quieted down, Jackie Jackson turned to Mike. "And, in the category of Ancient Greek Literature, here is your next question, Mr. Brady," he said. "From whence comes the expression that we often hear: Beware of Greeks bearing gifts?"

121

Mike looked at him disdainfully. "I'm going to assume that your information on that is incorrect," he said. "Scholarship has unearthed new facts that have not yet been published."

Jackson seemed to shrink a bit. "Oh," he replied weakly.

"Yes," Mike went on. "Your information probably tells you that the expression was one result of the incident involving the Greeks and the Trojans. As the myth has it, the Greeks after a long and unsuccessful seige of Troy, boarded their ship and apparently sailed for home, leaving a large wooden horse on the beach as a parting gift. The Trojans then supposedly moved the horse inside the walls of their city. And, that night, as the story goes, an army of Greeks emerged from the horse and—well, it gets a little messy after that, so I won't go into detail. In any event, hence the expression: Beware of Greeks bearing gifts. The implication being that any gift given by a person of Greek descent will be a booby trap."

"But that's not right?" Jackson asked, shaking his head.

"The true fact is—as will be revealed by J.R. P.N. Boatwistle, in his book *It's All Greek to Me*, to be published along about the close of this century—that in the original form of the expression, the term 'Greek' did not even appear."

"Son of a gun!" Jackson said, astonished.

"Yes. As J.R.P.N. Boatwistle tells us, the expression was first used in 1823 by one Luke (Hiram) Haystack, a farmer in Cumminroundaben, Ohio. It seems—"

"Cumminroundaben?"

"Named, of course, after the Cumminrounda-ben Indians."

"Oh, yeah . . . sure . . ." Jackson nodded, no doubt recalling the tribe.

"Haystack was sitting by the stream that ran through his property one day, fishing, when he saw a fair-sized wooden box, marked 'Danger!' and 'Dynamite!' floating toward him. Curious, he tossed a stone at it. The resulting explosion killed every fish for nearly a thousand miles around. And, later, asked to comment on the incident and draw some worthwhile conclusion, Haystack remarked, 'Beware of creeks bearing gifts.' "

Jackson looked dubious. "He said 'creeks'?"

"I know . . . he should have said 'stream,' " Mike replied. "But, remember, Haystack was an untutored farmer. It would be asking a bit much to expect him to know the technical difference between a stream and a creek."

"Gee . . . I wonder how it got twisted around," Jackson mused.

"I can explain that," Mike replied. "The newspaper reporter who asked him to comment on the incident and draw a worthwhile conclusion was hard of hearing. He thought Haystack had said 'Greek.' "

"But didn't he think that was a little funny? What did a Greek have to do with it?"

"That didn't interest the reporter," Mike replied. "All he knew was that he had to get the

123

story written and in to the paper before the deadline."

"It all begins to make sense," Jackson nodded. He got out his pencil again and did some scratching-out and scribbling on the card he was holding. Then he turned to the audience, which, like a single entity, was holding its breath, waiting for the verdict. "Ladies and gentlemen—that's right!" Jackson shouted. "The answer is: Hiram (Luke) Haystack!"

In his scholarly way, Mike winced. "Luke (Hiram) Haystack," he said, correcting Jackson.

When the horn honked, indicating that time had run out, both Carol and Mike had answered all the questions correctly. And this time when they were asked if they would return the following week there was no hedging, they agreed without any hesitation.

"We'd looooooooooooove it!" Carol squealed.

"I *have* to come back," Mike replied wittily. "This week I won the sky-diving lessons. Next week, I want to win the parachute!"

The audience roared.

When they left the theater after the show, they were set upon by a second collection of fans. They escaped with their clothes—and their lives—only by leaping into a cab and being driven, with doors locked, the one block to the garage where they had parked their car.

Driving home, they discussed their new status.

"It's idiotic!" Mike said. "Carol, we're not personalities! We're just fairly nice common ordinary people. This is a fantasy! It's not real!"

124

"I agree with you entirely," Carol replied. "I don't even know why we're doing it. We can only lose, in the long run. Mike, have you noticed what a strange place our home has become? I haven't really talked to any of the children since we got mixed up in this rat race. Oh, we exchange words every once in a while when we happen to pass in the hall, but we haven't 'talked'—know what I mean?"

"Do I? The same is true of me. I haven't even seen much of the children. I've been locked up in the den almost twenty-four hours a day. Really, it's absurd!"

"There's not even anything to gain," Carol said. "Oh, a few prizes, yes. But . . . what, for instance, do you plan to do with those sky-diving lessons?"

"Take them up and throw them out of a plane."

"Exactly. And what use do we have for a subscription to *Sheet Metal Management*, or those half-price tickets for the canoe excursion over Angostura Dam, or bleacher seats for the next Berkeley sit-in? Mike, the smartest thing we could do when we get home is phone Jackie Jackson and tell him that we've changed our minds, we won't be back next week."

"We'll do it," Mike nodded. "The second we reach the house, we'll go straight to the phone."

Carol sighed, relieved. "I'm glad that's over," she said. "You were right—it was fantasy. And the most fantastic thing about it was that Solomon I. Solaman. He almost convinced me that he could make us famous."

125

"And rich," Mike said. "The way he talks about 'famous,' it can be interpreted as 'rich.'" He shook his head in amused wonder. "I was pretty close to believing that he could do it, too," he admitted. "There's something about him that's . . . that's . . . well, it's . . . you know what I mean."

"Yes. He's . . . he's . . . he's . . . well, you expressed it perfectly. I agree with you. I think that if we'd given him half a chance he would have been able to do it."

"I didn't say that."

"Oh. Oh, I thought that was what you meant."

"I *was* thinking it," Mike said. "I didn't say it, but, as a matter of fact, I *was* thinking it. People like that, you know, can pull a lot of strings. They have them right at their fingertips. It's too bad we didn't give him a chance to see what he could do with us. After all—" He chuckled.

Carol giggled. "After all, what?"

"Well, I mean, facts are facts. We're a fairly attractive couple. I see nothing to be gained by lying to ourselves and saying we're not. If we're such stumblebums, how do we get all that applause?"

"That audience even applauds Jackie Jackson's cue cards," Carol pointed out.

"True. There is far less significance in that, however, than in the fact that Solomon I. Solaman took one look at us and spotted us as personalities."

"Good point," Carol nodded. "I have a lot of respect for Mr. Solaman."

"With excellent reason," Mike said. "He's never been wrong."

Carol looked at her watch. "Mike . . . won't it be a little late to call Jackie by the time we get home? I have a rule: Never telephone anybody after eight-thirty p.m."

"You're absolutely right," Mike replied. "I'll call him in the morning. Although, he probably sleeps late. Well . . . anyway, I'll call him the first chance I get . . . if I don't forget it." He was quiet for a moment. Then he added, "I'll be pretty busy, studying for next week's show . . . I could easily forget a thing like calling him."

"Well, that's par in the life of a personality," Carol said gaily. "Busy, busy, busy . . . forget, forget, forget . . ."

8.

When Mike left the master bedroom the next morning, headed for the kitchen, he found the way blocked by Greg, who was standing in the middle of the hallway, arms outstretched.

"Hi!" Mike grinned. "How goes it?" He started to walk around Greg. But his oldest son moved, getting into his path again. "What is it? A new fad?" Mike asked. "Is it supposed to replace long hair?"

"I want to talk to you," Greg explained.

"Oh! Oh—right! You know, Carol and I were talking about that just last night on the way home from the show," Mike said, standing instead of attempting to proceed. "She brought up the point that we don't 'talk' to you children anymore. We exchange words, she said, but we don't 'talk.' I agreed with her. You know what we're going to have to do one of these days real soon? We're going to have to have a—"

"—a talk," Greg agreed. "So, if you have a couple minutes . . ."

"Of course, I do," Mike told him, putting an arm around his shoulders and guiding him along the hallway toward the kitchen. "And I can't think of a better time than the present. We'll have breakfast together and talk. What's on your mind?"

"Well, in a way, I guess, it's this quiz show," Greg replied.

"How were we last night?"

"Oh, fine. Everybody said you were great."

Mike beamed. "No kidding? Who?"

"Me and Peter and Bobby."

"Oh."

"And Marcia and Jan and Cindy said Carol was great—in case she asks," Greg said.

"That makes it even, doesn't it? What did Alice have to say?"

"She said you were both great."

Mike chuckled. "A fence-sitter, eh? Well, it isn't important. Carol and I don't care. Oh, I mean, sure, it's nice to hear compliments. But it's not as if we were show business pros. People like that live on praise, you know. Listen, I'll tell you what you can do for me, though, Greg. If you happen to be alone with Alice sometime soon, see if you can pin her down on what she *really* thinks. You know, it's a shame that the critics don't revue guests on quiz shows. The business never knows where its next superstar is coming from. Why not from a show like 'Stunts & Stumpers'?"

"I guess so. Only—"

They had reached the kitchen. Along with

Carol and the other children, a stranger was seated at the table, eating. He was a slender young man with large glasses and an extremely serious expression. Alice was refilling his coffee mug.

"Oh, here he is," Carol said to the stranger. She waved to Mike. "Hi, dear!"

He responded with a general greeting to all, then addressed Carol. "I was just having a talk with Greg," he said. "He was telling me how great we were last night."

"The girls were just telling *me* the same thing —just before you came in!" Carol replied. "Can we believe them?"

"They're *our* children, aren't they?" Mike answered, seating himself. "If we can't get an honest opinion from our own children, who can we get one from?" He addressed Greg, who was sitting down, too. "If we'd laid a bomb, you'd have told us so—right?"

"Uh . . . well—"

"There you are," Mike said to Carol. He smiled at the stranger. " 'Morning."

"This is Mr. Skeen," Alice told Mike.

The young man rose slightly and extended a hand. "Mr. Brady . . . it's nice—"

"Anybody have a pencil?" Mike asked.

"You're not supposed to autograph it, darling, you're supposed to shake it," Carol said.

"Oh . . . that's right . . . sorry." Mike smiled. He took Skeen's hand and shook it. "It's getting so that any time anybody shoves anything at me I think I'm supposed to sign my name to it," he explained, apologizing. "Mr. Skeen? Are you with Jackie or with Sol?"

"Sol?" Carol asked, curious.

"So quickly? You forget? Solomon I. Solaman."

Carol shook her head. "He's not with either of them, darling. He's with *Architecture Today*. That's a magazine."

"I know what it is, Carol," Mike replied. "I'm an architect—at the present, anyway. In any event, it's my favorite magazine."

"I have an appointment for an interview, Mr. Brady," the young man said. "I made it with your appointments secretary."

"That's me," Alice told Mike. "How do you want your eggs this morning?"

"Uhhh . . . poached," Mike answered. He turned back to Mr. Skeen. "That's very flattering, *Architecture Today* wanting an interview with me," he said. "What slant did you have in mind? I have some fairly strong opinions, for one thing, on the current popularity of reinforced concrete construction. I was saying to a fellow architect just the other day that if they keep putting up concrete buildings at the rate they have been, all our cities are soon going to look like graveyards." He chuckled, then waited for Skeen and the others to respond to the remark in their individual ways.

They all stared at him blankly, as if waiting for him to continue.

"What I meant was, from the air, all the cities will look like one big graveyard. With a lot of tombstones," Mike explained.

As one, the others scowled, trying to bring the picture to mind.

"Perhaps I should have said, 'an aerial view from just the right angle,'" Mike said. "Anyway," he went on, addressing the visitor again, "speaking of angles, what angle exactly did you want to play up in this interview?"

"Well, my idea was to get your opinion on all the big questions of the day," Mr. Skeen replied. "What can we do to stop inflation, for instance. How can we solve the race problems. What can we do about closing the generation gap—that sort of thing."

The whole Brady bunch peered wide-eyed at Mr. Skeen.

"I'm . . . uh . . . I'm just an architect, Mr. Skeen," Mike replied dimly. "I don't know *every-thing*."

"Why would anybody want to read what Mike thinks about these problems?" Carol asked. "I mean, he might have some interesting opinions. But they're probably the same opinions everybody else has. And, he's just not much of an expert on those subjects."

"But he's known now," Mr. Skeen explained. "Our readers will see that the interview is with Mike Brady, and they'll say to themselves, 'Oh, yes, I *know* him.' Then they'll read it. It doesn't matter that he isn't an expert on social or monetary problems. What's important is that he's an architect, and we're an architectural magazine, and the architects who read us will be pleased to see that an architect has become well known

132

enough to be asked opinions about something other than architecture. Understand?"

The members of the Brady family shook their heads in unison.

Mr. Skeen looked mildly uncomfortable. "Let me put it another—"

He was interrupted by the ringing of the doorbell.

"That's the bell," Mike said to Alice.

"Is that your opinion as an architect or as a bigtime brass knocker and doorbell expert?" she asked, departing.

"See what I mean?" Mike said to Mr. Skeen. "People would only laugh if I tried to push off my opinions on those subjects on them."

"They'll only laugh if they don't agree with you, Mr. Brady," Skeen replied. "The ones who *do* agree with you will think you're brilliant. Besides, the important thing for you is that you'll be getting the publicity."

"Yes . . . well, I always say, uh, it doesn't matter what they say about you, just as long as, uh . . ." He turned to Carol. "What's the rest of that thing I always say?"

"Just as long as they spell your name right."

"It's B-r-a-d-y," Mike said to Skeen.

"I'm aware of that. Now, if—"

Alice had returned. "The Goodyear blimp and friend are in the living room," she announced. "They want to talk to Mr. and Mrs. Brady. And the blimp seems to be unaccustomed to being kept waiting."

133

"The Goodyear blimp?" Carol asked. "Alice, are you—oh! It's Solomon I. Solaman!"

"That's what *he* claims," Alice replied. "But if I didn't see him floating around over the Rose Bowl last January, I'm not as qualified to write an article on lighter-than-air aircraft as I think I am."

"Alice, if that's a crack at me—" Mike began. But he decided he had no more time to waste on a retort. "Honey," he said to Carol, "we better not keep Sol waiting." Rising, he spoke to Skeen. "We probably won't be long," he said. "Sol is a busy man, he won't have much time for us. In the meantime, have another breakfast." Then, leaving the table, he halted and patted Greg on the shoulder. "Glad we could have that talk," he said. "Any time you want to talk again, my door is always open."

"Your door is always locked—you're in there studying," Alice told him.

" 'Door is always open' is just a figure of speech," Mike explained. Then he and Carol hurried out, headed for the living room.

Solomon I. Solaman sat down as they entered the room. "I'm a busy man," he said crossly. "Please don't dawdle the next time I send for you. I should have had you come to my office, but I wanted to see your home. I thought we might be able to use it in some way to promote you as personalities. But, as homes go, it's very—" His nose twitched, as if he had smelled something rancid. "—very ordinary. Too bad you don't have a house built out of junked boxcars. It would even be better if you lived in a cave instead of a house.

As it is, however—" He shuddered, dismayed. "Well, let's move on to pleasanter thoughts." He indicated the tall, middle-aged, well-dressed, brisk-looking man who was standing near his chair. "This is Walter W. Walter," he said. "He's an advertising man. And he has a proposition to make us. I have already accepted it on our behalf. But I find that it adds to the efficiency if my clients know what I've agreed for them to do. Mr. Walker will explain."

"Walter, not Walker," Walter W. Walter said to Solomon I. Solaman.

"Yes . . . well, whatever the name is. Please explain the proposition to . . . to, uh . . . to those two," he said, pointing to Mike and Carol.

Walter grinned cheerily. "Hi, kids!" he waved. "What Mr. Solaman didn't mention was that, as an ad man, I represent the Many Splendored Thing chain of chopped meat dispensaries—or, as they're referred to by the general public, 'hamburger stands.' As you undoubtedly know, the motto at Many Splendored Thing is A New Flavor Every Month!' What that means is that every month we put a new flavor on the market. We've been in business for five years and, so far, true to our word, we have sixty-one flavors. That's one more flavor than there are months in five years, you say. And you are correct. But remember, we had one flavor when we started out—the hamburger-flavored hamburger. Since then, we've added such delicacies as the peanut burger, spinach burger, marshmallow burger, leather burger, cherry burger, liver burger, rose petal burger, and monkey bar burger. It's getting a little difficult, in fact, to find flavors to add to the line. And, continuing to be totally frank, we find that the public no longer pays much attention when we add a new flavor. We introduced the Sea of Tranquillity burger last month—in recognition, of course, of all the current interest in the moon—and it didn't even raise a yawn."

"Which brings us to the problem," Solomon I. Solaman said.

"Yes," Walter W. Walter agreed. "We must either think up a new ad campaign to add zip to sales, or we must add zip to the old campaign to get around the necessity for thinking up a new campaign. And, since we're a little short on ideas, we've decided to stick with the old idea—but give it a little boosty-woosty." He winked. "In other words, a tie-in," he went on. "We want to hitch our hamburger to your star. Our flavor for next month will be the pomegranate burger. And we want to associate it with you—Mike and Carol Brady—in the minds of the general public. When they think of Mike and Carol, we want them to think of the Many Splendored Thing pomegranate burger!" He sighed ecstatically. "Makes the old heart strings twang, don't it?"

"Thrilling," Solomon I. Solaman murmured glumly. "Tell them what is expected of them."

"Here's the pitch," Walter W. Walter said to Mike and Carol, working up enthusiasm. "You two will be on hand when the first pomegranate burger rolls off the assembly line. Mike, you'll add the onion, and Carol, you'll douse it with catsup. We'll have the mayor there—the governor, if possible. We'll shoot pictures, of course. There'll be newspaper publicity. We'll have it on the TV news shows. Radio will cover, naturally—although—continuing the vein of frankness —a hamburger doesn't show up too well on radio."

"In short, the same old jazz," Solomon I. Solaman said, rising. "Shall we go now, Wolper?"

"Walter," Walter said, correcting him. "Yes, I think that pretty much sums it up."

"But—" Mike began.

"Of course!" Walter W. Walter broke in. "You want to know how this will benefit you. I knew I'd left something out. As soon as the publicity peters out, you see, we intend to hit with a big advertising and promotion campaign. We'll have TV commercials—you and Carol telling the general public how you lived on Many Splendored Thing pomegranate burgers while you crammed for the questions on 'Stunts & Stumpers.' We'll have full-page ads in the newspapers—you and Carol wheeling into a Many Splendored Thing stand, and balloons over your heads with writing on them, revealing that you have pomegranate burgers on your minds. Fantastic! It's all free— all that exposure. We won't be charging you a cent."

"Not to mention the free pomegranate burgers," Solomon I. Solaman said, floating toward the exit.

"Well . . . maybe not free," Walter W. Walter said, tagging after him. "How about half-price?"

"We'll negotiate it," Solomon I. Solaman said, departing.

Left by themselves, Mike and Carol looked at each other.

"Of all the things that have happened so far, that was the most preposterous," Mike said. "We didn't get a chance to say a word."

"I guess Sol thinks he knows what's best for us," Carol replied.

"Well, I don't know about you, but I have no intention of endorsing a pomegranate burger." He headed back toward the kitchen. "And the next time I see Sol, I intend to tell him so."

"I agree with you," Carol said. "Why don't you call his office and leave a message? Although, he probably has one of those machines that records incoming calls, and he probably never gives it a chance to tell him who called, let alone what they said."

"I'll tell him in person, the next time I see him. Anyway, I don't have time to phone him right now. *Architecture Today* is waiting to find out how to handle inflation."

They reached the kitchen and Mike took Mr. Skeen to the den with him.

"Isn't Mike wonderful!" Carol said to the children. "I don't think he knows a thing about inflation, and yet he's willing to take the time to give that magazine writer his views."

"Do you think it will take very long?" Greg asked.

"Why, dear?"

"I still want to talk to him," Greg explained.

"Again? Darling, you two just finished one long talk. You can't expect him to be on call every minute of the day. What's your problem? Is it anything I can help you with?"

Greg shook his head. "I guess not," he replied sadly. Then he left the table.

Peter followed him. And after Peter had gone, Bobby got up and left.

Carol spoke to Alice. "Alice, make an appointment for Mike to talk to the boys soon," she said. "I think it might be important."

"And how about an appointment for you to talk to the girls?" Alice said.

Carol looked at Marcia, then Jan, then Cindy. "Problems?" she asked.

"Yes," Marcia replied. "Mom, it's that TV show!"

"Oh, you don't have to tell *me* that!" Carol said. "In fact, I'm sure you're not aware of even half the problems connected with that TV show. Come along," she said, leaving the kitchen, "I have to make a few phone calls, and, between calls, I'll tell you about some of the probems. For instance," she went on, going out the door, "we are now face-to-face with another crisis. To endorse the pomegranate burger or not to endorse the pomegranate burger, that is the question—"

The girls remained at the table, letting Carol proceed alone. She did not return, so they guessed that she did not realize that they were not with her.

"Maybe if we called her on the phone we could talk to her," Jan said.

"You wouldn't get her," Alice told her. "The line is always busy."

"If we had a quiz program, I bet Mom'd talk to uth," Cindy said. "Do we have enough in our thavingth to buy one?"

"Alice . . . what are we going to do?" Marcia asked plaintively. "Mike and Mom are so wrapped up in 'Stunts & Stumpers' these days, they don't know that anything else is going on in the world."

"Or any*body* else, either," Jan complained.

"Oh, I don't know," Alice replied. "Mike seems to be keeping up. He has the solution to inflation, the race problems and the generation gap—all on the tip of his tongue. Tell you what," she said, "let's give them a little more rope. One of these weeks, one of them is going to miss a question on that quiz show. And where will they be then? Mike will be back at the office, and Carol will be back in her home."

"I'm not so sure," Marcia said gloomily. "I think they *like* this. All this run, run, run, go, go, go, do, do, do. I have sort of a theory. I think maybe before they were a little tired of us and all our problems and this is their escape. They're getting away from us, you have to admit that. We can't talk to them, we don't even get much chance to see them."

"Of course, there might be another angle to it," Alice said. "Do you think that perhaps you and the boys are a little bit jealous? For once, you're not getting all the attention."

The girls exchanged looks.

"That's an idea . . . sort of . . ." Marcia said.

"I'm not saying it's true," Alice told them. "But, think about it. You're right, Mike and Carol aren't thinking about much of anything—or any*one*— except themselves these days. Maybe they're not the only ones who are making that mistake, though." She smiled encouragingly. "Why don't you girls talk it over with the boys? See what you decide."

Once more, the girls exchanged looks. Then they got up and trooped out.

"And find out what Tiger and Fluffy think about it, too!" Alice called after them. "You might be surprised by what you can learn from . . . oh, never mind." The girls had passed beyond the range of her voice.

9.

The audience exploded in a frenzy of cheers. Again, Mike and Carol had answered every question correctly on "Stunts & Stumpers"! Mike was standing beside Jackie Jackson smiling thinly, looking obviously bored, as the studio audience and the viewers wanted their favorite scholar and wit to look. And Carol was flitting about the stage, throwing kisses to the cameramen, the director, the announcer, the audience—just as she was expected to do, being an adorable flutterhead. Then Jackie Jackson, teeth agleam, escorted them offstage. But the cheering, the stomping, the whistling, lingered on.

"My jaws are killing me," Carol complained. "You're lucky," she said to Mike. "They don't expect anything from you but an occasional sneer. But I have to do all that insane *grinning!*"

Mike had no chance to reply. He and Carol and Jackie Jackson were suddenly surrounded by fans who had stampeded past "Pop," the theater's lovable old doorman, and penetrated to the wings. They demanded autographs. For another half to three-quarters of an hour, Mike, Carol and Jackie Jackson remained captives, signing their names to anything and everything presented to them. When the final autograph had been scrawled, they limped to Jackie Jackson's office.

There, waiting for them, were Solomon I. Solaman and Walter W. Walter. The two visitors were accompanied by a young man who was loaded down with photographic equipment.

"Let's get right down to business," Solomon I. Solaman said to them, "already nearly three-thousandths of a second of my exceedingly valuable time have been wasted. Now, I am here to announce that I have lined up another new venture for you. In the meantime, Mr. Wombat will fill you in on the progress of the tie-in with Many Splendored Thing."

"That's Walter, not Wombat," Walter W. Walter said, correcting Solaman. Then he turned to Mike and Carol. "We want to get some relaxed, casual shots to use in the publicity," he said. "That's why Hal, my photographer, is here. Listen, kids, just act natural, you know? Try to imagine that Hal isn't even here. That's why I didn't introduce him to you. I want you to think of him as the invisible man—got it?"

A flashbulb went off.

Carol and Mike blinked. "If he's the invisible man, where is the flashing coming from?" Mike grumbled.

"Did I say his camera was invisible?"

"Attention—over here!" Solomon I. Solaman called, rapping on Jackson's desk. "Regarding the new venture, we're calling it 'The Mike & Carol Show.' It'll be a Mr. & Mrs. You know the kind of gunk they put on TV in the morning—sort of thing. It will be televised directly from your home. I got the idea for the show when I visited your house. 'Good heavens!' I said, reacting in horror, 'this is the sort of atrocious abode from which they televise those terrible Mr. & Mrs. shows!' I went straight to the network with the idea and got a turn-down on the spot."

"Mike . . . try to look casual with a pomegranate burger," Walter said.

"I don't have a pomegranate burger!"

"Fake it," Walter said. "Nobody has a pomegranate burger yet. It won't be introduced until the first of the month. At the moment, it's still on the drawing board. Our engineering department is having a bit of trouble fitting it into the Many Splendored Thing cost accounting system, profit-and-losswise." He fashioned a view-finder from his fingers and peered at Mike and Carol. "Essentially, what I want," he told them, "is vigorous relaxation."

"How about me in the picture?" Jackie Jackson suggested. "I'm their best friend."

"Nahhhh . . . I'm afraid of the teeth," Walter replied. "They pick up too much reflection."

"I got a shot where I bounce the flash off the wall," the photographer told Walter. "I could probably bounce it off the teeth instead."

Walter shook his head. "I didn't want to say it,

144

but frankly the teeth would draw attention away from the pomegranate burger."

"However," Solomon I. Solaman went on, addressing Mike and Carol, "the network is very aware of the fact that I have never been wrong. So, we came to an arrangement. The show will be seen only locally for the first week or so. If it's a hit—and we all know it will be, because Solomon I. Solaman has never been wrong—it will go network. Now, you do have children, don't you?"

"Six," Carol replied.

"Make it two," Solaman advised. "Six names are too many for the homemakers at home to remember. Don't forget, our audience will be made up of every lamebrain in the country. Remembering how to switch on the set is about the limit of their intellectual abilities."

"But the viewers will probably see all six of them," Mike said. "How can we distribute two names among six children? Three children to each name?"

"The children will *not* be seen," Solomon I. Solaman told him. "You'll only *talk* about them. Your home is supposed to be a *typical* home. People in typical homes don't *see* their children. They only *talk* about them—mostly to complain."

A half-dozen flashbulbs went off in rapid succession, causing Mike and Carol first to claw the air, as if they had been attacked by a horde of swooping bats, and then to cover their eyes with their hands, handicapped by temporary blindness.

"Wonderful!" Walter enthused. "Now, that's

what I call *involved* relaxation! Only, next time, don't wave your arms. Just try to *suggest* arm-waving by the way you roll your eyes. Got it?"

One of the ushers appeared in the doorway and motioned to Jackie Jackson and the m.c. left the office and began a low-voiced conversation with the usher in the corridor.

"Your maid is good, though," Solaman told Mike and Carol. "We'll keep her in. Will she need a writer or does she do her own stuff?"

"Well, so far, she's managed to run the house pretty well without a writer," Mike replied. "What do you mean, a writer? Isn't this one of those off-the-cuff things? I thought we'd just be sitting there at the breakfast table, talking, the way we do every morning."

"Exactly," Solomon I. Solaman nodded. "But you don't expect to grab off a respectable rating with the kind of drivel that normally passes for conversation at your breakfast table, do you?"

"How do you know what kind of drivel passes for conversation at our breakfast table!" Mike responded angrily.

"Temperament," Solaman sighed sorrowfully. "The distinguishing mark of the personality—the childish resort to a temper tantrum . . ."

"Just answer the question!" Mike insisted. "When did you ever have breakfast with us?"

"I've never been to the bottom of the ocean, either," Solaman replied. "But I blessed well know it's down there! If it weren't, all the water would run out!"

Mike and Carol looked at each other.

"You can't argue with that," Carol said.

Mike nodded and retreated into a kind of self-induced coma.

"That's it! That's it!" Walter cried excitedly, dancing around Mike. "That's the look I want—vigorous relaxation—and he's doing it without moving an arm!"

The office was lighted by a barrage of flash-bulb explosions.

"You go on the air at nine tomorrow morning, directly from your breakfast table," Solomon I. Solaman told Mike and Carol. "Rehearsal will be at five a.m. I'll expect you to be up and bright-eyed."

"Right—the way we are typically at five a.m.," Carol replied.

"Don't disappoint the network," Solomon I. Solaman said, departing. "It has faith in Solomon I. Solaman."

"Now, Carol," Walter said, "if we could just get the same expression from you—the old vigorous relaxation."

"Hold it!" Jackie Jackson said, coming back into the office. "If what I heard is true, this whole deal could go down the drain. I just got it from a confidential but reliable source—"

"That usher, you mean?" Mike asked.

"No names!" Jackie Jackson said, near panic. "Do you want to jeopardize me with my stool pigeons?"

Mike went to the office doorway and looked out. "He's gone," he reported.

"Okay, then, in answer to your question, yes,

147

that usher," Jackson said. "But he isn't just an usher. He's a spy for Buck Artwald, the TV col-columnist on the *Post-Observer-Times*. Artwald planted him here to spy on me."

"But he also spies on Buck Artwald for you?" Mike guessed.

"Yeah . . . well, spying doesn't pay so well, he's got to do a little moonlighting," Jackson replied. "But, here's the tragedy: Artwald has been watching you two on the show, and he's got the idea in his head that 'Stunts & Stumpers' is fixed!"

"That's terrible!" Carol responded.

"Well, it's natural," Jackson said. "You two just keep on answering questions, week after week. It's not human. And, too, he's heard about the build-up that Solomon I. Solaman's giving you. So, he figures that your appearance on 'Stunts & Stumpers' is just part of the whole ball of wax. It has me worried, believe me. If it got into his column in the *P-O-T* that I'm running a rigged quiz show, I'd be dead in the business. After my last show folded, I was years getting another spot, you know."

"Was that for—" Mike began.

"—running a rigged quiz show," Jackson nodded. "But that was okay. Nobody held it against me. *Everybody* was running a rigged quiz show in those days."

"Then why did it take you so long to get another spot?" Carol asked.

"When I said 'nobody' held it against me, I didn't mean 'nobody.' Only the people in the business, I meant. They understood. Why wouldn't they? They were running rigged quiz shows, too. But they couldn't put me back on the air. Because the people in the audience weren't like the people in the business—they didn't understand. So, putting me back on the air would have been bad business. People in the business understand that even more—good business from bad business. Understand?"

"No," Mike replied. "But there *is* one thing I want to be sure I do understand. *This* quiz show isn't rigged, is it?"

Jackson shook his head and raised his left hand. "On my honor!" he said. "I'll do even better than that—on the Boy Scouts' honor!" He lowered the hand. "There's no need to fix the show," he said. "You both know all the answers, anyway."

"Then what are you worried about?" Carol asked.

"That won't stop Artwald from hinting that the show is fixed," Jackson explained. "And if you read in his column in the *P-O-T* that the show was gimmicked, and you'd seen you two answering all those hard questions, and you knew that a certain m.c.—no names—had a history that included a rigged quiz show, what would you think?"

"You're right—you got a problem," Mike told him.

"*I* got a problem? *We* got a problem. If they investigate me, they'll investigate you. There goes your whole career as a personality. Cheaters never win, you know."

"But they can't prove it!" Carol protested. "We haven't cheated!"

"Who'd believe it?" Jackson replied. He turned to Walter. "Do *you* believe it?"

Walter looked at Mike and Carol suspiciously. "Ahhhh . . . about the tie-in with Many Splendored Thing . . ." he said. ". . . let's let it hang loose for the nonce. I'll be . . . ahhh . . ." He motioned to the photographer. "Come on, Hal . . ." At the doorway, he paused a second. "Don't call me," he said to Mike and Carol. "I'll call you." Then he was gone.

"See what I mean?" Jackson said to them. "He *knows* you didn't cheat, but he doesn't believe it. What he believes is that you're just like him—rotten to the core. He is what I would call a truly typical citizen."

Mike shook his head. "Sorry, I don't believe it."

"You'll believe it when you find out you can't sleep tonight, worrying about your career," Jackie Jackson told him.

"How would it hurt me as an architect?" Mike asked.

"Not that career," Jackson replied. "I mean your *real* career, as a personality."

"And speaking of that," Carol said. "We better get home and try to get some sleep, dear. Five o'clock in the morning is going to be here awfully soon."

"You're right," Mike agreed, moving toward the doorway. "I wonder what Sol meant by 'writers,'" he said, as he and Carol hurried along the corridor. "I suppose we could use some lead-ins to the commercials. But, as for the patter, I think that should be strictly our own, don't you? I mean, wasn't that what sold the network on trying this show in the first place? Oh, sure, Sol went to them with the idea, but if the network boys hadn't caught our act on 'Stunts & Stumpers,' how far would he have got with it? My point is, basically, it was Mike and Carol who put us across— am I right?"

"Only a thousand per cent," Carol replied. "Honey, now that you mention it, here's something to think about: How much do we really *need* Sol?"

When Mike and Carol reached home, they found Alice and the six children and cat and dog lined up inside the doorway.

"What a won-der-fullllllll reception!" Carol whooped, advancing through the ambush, kissing all the children. "And we know what you want to tell us—that we were fantastic and marvelous, as usual. But darlings—and you, too, Alice and Fluffy and Tiger—I must get to bed! If I don't get my beauty sleep, well, it just might mean the end of civilized society, as we know it. Mike will explain it to you—ta-ta!"

She went dashing off toward the master bedroom.

"We have a little surprise for you," Mike told Alice and the children and the pets. "We'll be having company along about five in the morning —cameramen and their cameras and a director

151

and a script girl—I think that's the phrase—and all the little people who're necessary to putting a TV show on the air. What I'm getting at is—" He told them about the Mr. & Mrs. show.

"Will *we* be on it?" Cindy asked, wide-eyed.

"Actually, no," Mike replied. "According to the script, as I understand it, Carol and I have only two children. And they're neither seen nor heard."

"Which two?" Cindy asked. "Me and Jan or me and Marcia?"

"Well, ah, when I said 'two,' what I meant was—"

"Not girls!" Bobby broke in. "If they had only two kids, they wouldn't have *any* girls."

"Bobby!" Alice said.

"Don't blame me," he replied. "I'm just telling you how Dad feels about it."

"I didn't say that," Mike protested. "Of course I'd have girls."

"Two?" Peter asked. "If you had only two children and they were both girls, that would mean no boys. Is *that* what you meant?"

Mike was backing away. "Alice . . . explain it to them . . ." he said. "It's almost time for me to get up, and I haven't even been to bed yet." He turned and hurried along the hallway toward the bedroom.

"Is that what he meant?" Peter asked Alice. "If he had a choice, did he mean, he wouldn't have any boys?"

"What'th tho thurprithing about that?" Cindy asked.

"That is *not* what he meant," Alice assured Peter. "What he meant—though he probably didn't realize it—is 'that this whole thing has gone far enough. He would never have said anything like that before. And if he *had* said it, he'd have stayed around to *un*say it!" She looked into the faces of the children. "Mike and Carol have been bitten by the show business bug," she told them. "And we better do something about it before the bite becomes a full-scale epidemic. If *that* happens, life around here will be like this permanently. Who has an idea?"

The question was met with painful silence.

"Well . . . maybe I know a way out," Alice said. "There's an old saying that fits this situation. It goes: Nine can play the same game, or, What's show business for the parents is show business for the maid, the six children and the dog and cat."

The children looked wholly baffled.

Alice spread her arms. "Let's huddle," she said. "And let's make it fast—we have to be up at five in the morning."

10.

Mike was awakened the next morning not by the alarm clock but by an alarming banging on the front door. His eyes flew open. He stared into space for a second, and then he scrambled out of bed, intending to find out who or what was engaged in knocking down the front door. As he was striding from the bedroom, the alarm began ringing. Quickly, he turned and ran back, instinctively needing to silence it. But he was still not quite fully awake, and he lost his bearings and took a shortcut across the bed, head-first. By this time, of course, Carol was awake and sitting up. Naturally, she was curious about why Mike had apparently slept crosswise on the bed and why the alarm was ringing and the front door was being battered in at the same time.

"I'm not sure," Mike told her, "but I think we're warming up the audience for the main show—the way the comic does for Jackie Jackson."

Carol remembered. "The show! The Mr. & Mrs. show! That must be the TV people at the—"

The pounding on the front door had stopped.

"They're going away!" Carol said in panic, leaping out of bed. "They think we're not home and they're going away. They're going to find some other Mr. & Mrs. to be on the show!"

"Carol—"

She was racing toward the bedroom doorway. She reached it just as a young man—a stranger—appeared in the opening. From the top down, the young man was dressed in a ten-gallon hat (white), an orange silk shirt decorated with yellow daisies, riding breeches and riding boots, and he was carrying a riding whip. Carol skidded to a halt in front of him. Then she screamed and whipped around and dashed to the closet and dived in. The door closed behind her.

Mike and the stranger stared at the closet door.

A few seconds later, it opened. Carol stepped out, now wearing a robe. "Well, good morning all!" She smiled gaily.

"Top 'o," the young man replied, cracking his riding whip. "I assume you're my stars. I'm your director—Danny Daniel."

"Was that *you* doing all that pounding?" Mike asked. "How did you get in?"

"It was me doing the tapping, yes," Danny Daniel replied. "And I was greeted—finally—by the delightful Alice, grown at last, and some of her friends from Wonderland. The Munchkins, I believed they're called."

"That's Oz," Carol told him.

"Oh? Well, she told me her name was Alice. Be that as it may, it was she who let me in. And, while the technicians are setting up the equipment, I thought I'd look for a nice quiet spot for the writers to hibernate. They *demand* quiet, you know. Could we have this room cleared for them?"

"This is our bedroom," Mike told him.

"Oh, they won't mind. They prefer second-class quarters, as a matter of fact. Great fuel for all their guilt complexes." He beamed. "Well now, stars! Up and at'em! On the set!" He cracked the whip. "First rehearsal in five minutes!" Then he disappeared from the opening, heading back toward the main part of the house.

Mike quickly closed the door. "Oh, he's going to be a sweetheart," he grumbled, as he and Carol began to dress. "Cracking that whip all over the place . . . If he hits any of the children, out he goes!"

"Now, Mike, don't be—"

The bedroom door opened. A small, dumpy, middle-aged man with rimless glasses and dressed in a rumpled, out-of-fashion suit stood in the opening. Again, Carol screamed and fled to the closet.

"Hi ya," the man said to Mike. "I'm your head writer. Who was the . . . uh, lady?"

"That 'lady' you just saw was my wife!" Mike replied sharply.

The head writer grinned broadly. "Hey! I think you've got the basis for a great joke there with that line," he said. "It's okay, lady," he called out, entering the room. "I got a wife of my own, so you go right on ahead and dress." He dropped into a bedroom chair, pushed it back, and raised his legs, resting his feet on a small occasional table.

The closet door opened a crack and Carol peeked out. "Who are you?" she demanded.

"He's our head writer, dear," Mike explained. He turned back to the writer. "You didn't mention your name."

"And I won't either, until I see how the show goes," the writer replied. "If the ratings are good, I'll tell you who I am. If not, what difference does it make? You'll never see me again, anyway." He addressed Carol again. "It's okay," he told her. "You won't embarrass me."

"*That* is not what I'm worried about," Carol replied. "I'll just dress in here." The door closed.

"What's it like being married to a modesty nut?" the writer asked Mike.

Mike ignored him, continuing to dress.

"Do you have any suggestions for a close?" the writer asked.

Mike halted the process of buttoning his shirt. "For a what?"

"A close," the writer replied. "You know that line at the end of the show? The camera always zeroes in on the star—that's you and your lady friend—and you come out with this closing line. Like, uh, 'God bless.' Or 'Keep those cards and letters coming in.' Any ideas?"

Mike shook his head and continued the buttoning process.

"It's the most important part of the show," the writer told him. "What goes before—who cares? But the close, that's the star's signature. It

157

sums him up. It tells the audience exactly what kind of guy he is. I'll tell you the perfect show: Twenty-nine minutes and fifty-seven seconds of total silence and total darkness, and then three seconds for the closing line. A show like that would never wear out its welcome."

"Fine, fine," Mike murmured, trying not to pay attention.

Carol emerged from the closet, dressed. She waggled her fingers at the writer. "Hi!"

"I was just telling your friend about a great closing line I thought up," the writer said to her. "The star waves a fond good-bye to the viewers, and he says: 'Now, everybody—go stick your foot in the ice cream freezer.' I've been trying to sell that line to stars and directors and producers for fifteen years. Nobody will buy it. They're afraid of the censors. They think there's something unclean about it."

"What?" Carol asked, perplexed, not having heard the rest of the conversation.

"Never mind," Mike said to her. "Let's go!" He got her by the hand and led her toward the doorway.

"How's 'Bye, folks!' for a close?" the writer called after them.

Mike shut the door behind them. Then they walked down the hallway toward the kitchen.

"What was he talking about?" Carol asked.

"Believe me, you're better off not knowing," Mike replied. "I wonder if we get breakfast before we start this breakfast show or if we have to wait until it's on before we eat breakfast."

"I don't know what *you're* talking about any more even!" Carol said, a touch of panic in her tone.

They reached the kitchen and breakfast area. Technicians were everywhere, setting up equipment. Sprinkled among them, at the breakfast table or wandering about, were Alice and the children.

"Do you know what time it is?" Mike demanded, entering the kitchen. "What are you all doing up?"

"Getting paid overtime," a technician replied.

"Not you—them!" Mike said, indicating the children. He addressed Alice. "They're supposed to be in bed," he said.

"With all that pounding going on?" Alice replied. "Anyway, the boys' room is now the office of the assistant director. And the director himself is in the girls' room."

"What's he doing in there?" Mike protested.

"Supervising," Alice replied. "The telephone company is in there putting in telephones for him. Seven telephones. I think he's expecting a call."

Mike sat down at the table. "Coffee-black," he ordered.

Carol sat down also. "Two," she said dimly.

"Nyet!" a voice roared. Danny Daniel appeared. "Nyet! Nyet! No food. We'll be on the air in a few hours. No food before the performance. It's an old show biz superstition—like not whistling in the dressing room. Ask any old show biz vet and he'll tell you: Never eat on an empty stomach." He sat down at the table with Mike and Carol and the two children who were there, Greg and Jan. "Great news!" he said, addressing Mike and Carol. "Really fabulous news. The telephone company is going to let me have eight phones instead of just seven."

"That *is* wonderful." Mike nodded.

"I have a telephone under my pillow now," Jan told them.

"Oh . . . is that *your* pillow?" Danny Daniel said. "Listen, hon, any calls that come in during the night, just take a message." He turned his attention to Mike and Carol again. "Who are all these little people running around the house?" he asked.

"Those are the children," Carol told him.

"Children?" He chuckled. "Don't tell me those are children." He shook his head. "I have children. And they're nothing at all like these little people. Children shriek. Children are constantly demanding things. They always want to play with daddy's whip. Children are naughtykins. They dump their oatmeal in daddy's boots. These little people you have around here are *not* children. I *know* what children are. Not only do *I* have children, but I also have close friends who have children. And their children are just like my children. Take it from me, stars, these little people you have running around your house are not children. I suspect that someone passed off a bunch of midgets on you."

Mike was shaking his head. "They're children," he insisted.

"Well . . . if they are, they certainly lack believability," Danny Daniel told him. His expression suddenly turned fearful. "You don't intend to put any of them on the show, do you?"

Mike shook his head. "Solomon I. Solaman ruled them out."

"Because Solomon I. Solaman is never wrong," a voice said. And at the same time Solomon I. Solaman appeared and joined them at the table. "How does it look?" he asked Danny Daniel.

"I think we'll be safe if we can just keep the little people off-camera," Daniel replied. "They worry me. I heard one of them say 'excuse me' a while ago. And another one said 'thank you.' It gives the whole atmosphere a sort of fantasy effect. But if one of them wandered on-camera and said something like that, the critics would roast us to high heaven. I mean, they'd say it was staged. Keep the little people out of the scene and I think we can squeeze by."

"If we get a good rating today, tomorrow we'll pack them off to a boarding school," Solomon I. Solaman promised him.

"I'd rest easier."

"Hold it!" Mike said. "The children stay right here!"

"Temperament again!" Solomon I. Solaman shuddered. "He doesn't even have the first show under his belt yet, and already he's acting like a star! Is it any wonder I can't abide personalities!" He rose. "I'll be in your office," he told Daniel. "I'm expecting some calls."

"I've got the phones for it," Daniel replied

proudly. As Solomon I. Solaman departed, he turned back to Mike and Carol. "Before I forget it, I better give you your personality assignments," he said. "Mike, you'll be a little grouchy this morning. You were probably up until the wee hours of the morning playing poker—and you had lou-zee cards. So, naturally, you blame it all on Carol. Husband-like, you know. You are very snappish with Carol. And, Carol, dear, you're playing it a little cagey—got that? Walking a tightrope, so to speak. Because you suspect that if you say one wrong thing, Mike will haul off and belt you one right in the kisser. The ladies in the audience will be able to identify with that. That's the way their husbands are *every* morning."

"I don't believe that," Carol replied.

"Take my word for it," Danny Daniel assured her. "That's the way *my* wife's husband is. And I consider her typical. "He turned his attention to Greg and Jan, who were looking on wide-eyed and open-eared. "Why don't you two midgets go report to your agents," he suggested amiably. "You don't want to get caught here when the show goes on, you know."

"Children, maybe it would be best if you stood back out of everybody's way," Carol said.

"Yes, ma'am," Greg replied, rising.

"All right, Mother," Jan said.

The two children departed, moving to the other side of the kitchen, where Alice was handing out cups of coffee to the technicians and the other

162

children were watching as the equipment was being installed.

"Did you hear that?" Danny Daniel said to Mike and Carol. "'Yes, ma'am!' 'All right, Mother!' Phony! They must be from some other century. You know what a *real* child says when you ask it to do something? It says, 'Go stick your foot in the ice cream freezer.' Always the same answer. I don't know where they pick up language like that. Well, anyway," he said, rising, "try to relax. And, meanwhile, Mike, work yourself up into a good grouch. I'll see you later—I want to go watch Solomon I. Solaman use my phones. It'll be a nice little name-dropping incident to use when I write my autobiography. Ta-ta!"

"Boy, he's right," Mike said, watching Danny Daniel depart, "the atmosphere around here sure has a fantasy effect all right. He's it."

"Did you hear what Solomon I. Solaman said about the children—send them to a boarding school!" Carol said. "He can't do that without our permission, can he?"

"Are you serious?"

"Well . . . he's our manager. And, so far, he's done everything else without our permission."

The head writer joined them at the table. "I got your closing line for you," he said. "It comes in two parts. Carol, you get the first part, and Mike, you get the second part. Carol, yours is 'So.' Mike you follow that up with 'long.' Think you can remember that?"

Mike stared at him. "You *wrote* that?"

The writer glanced about, making sure no one else was close enough to hear. "I'll be truthful with you," he said, speaking softly. "Only the 'so' is original. The 'long' I stole. It's from Shakespeare. But, believe me, nobody in *your* audience will recognize it." He rose and winked. "Keep it under your hats," he said. Then he headed back toward his office, the master bedroom.

Mike covered his face with his hands.

"Dear . . ."

"Could I be alone for a while?" he pleaded, still hiding behind his hands.

"Are you working up a grouch?"

"I've already reached it," Mike replied grimly. "I'm afraid if I'm not left alone I'll go right past it, straight on to a rage."

Carol got up and tiptoed away.

Danny Daniel returned from watching Solomon I. Solaman use his telephones at one minute before air time. Carol arrived back at the table at the same time. By then, Mike had managed to pull back from the brink of the rage to a position approximating a mild grouch. He had acquired a notepad and a pencil in the meantime and was doodling figures.

"Here's the opening," Daniel told Mike and Carol. "The camera will 'discover' you at the breakfast table. Understand? We won't have a formal opening—no announcer bringing you on like the Kentucky Derby or a Presidential address. Just 'old shoe'—got it? There you'll be, discussing common ordinary everyday things—the play opening you attended last night, the snack you had with the Duke and Duchess afterward, that sort of thing. Okay?" He pointed off-camera. "What are *they* doing over there?"

Mike and Carol looked where he was pointing and saw Alice and the six children and the dog and cat lined up behind one of the large lights.

"They're watching," Carol explained to Daniel. "They look ominous."

"They look normal to me," Mike said crossly.

"I thought they were being sent to a boarding school."

"That's not until tomorr—they're not going to a boarding school!" Carol told him.

"My contract definitely calls for jurisdiction over—" Daniel threw up his hands. "There's just not time to discuss it now." He pointed toward a camera. "When I want you to begin," he said, "I'll signal to you, and, at the same time, a red light will go on over there. Clear?"

"It isn't our first time on TV," Carol told him haughtily.

"I forgot. All right . . . twenty seconds . . ." Danny Daniel told them, backing out of camera range.

As the director withdrew, Mike pointed to the figures on the notepad. "See this?" he said, pointing to a number. "This is the value of the prizes we've won on 'Stunts & Stumpers.'"

"Oh—that's nice!" Carol replied, surprised. "I didn't realize it was so much."

"It's not as good as it looks," Mike said.

Danny Daniel signaled to them. The red light went on. But neither Carol nor Mike were aware of the signal from the director or the camera.

"Why? What's the problem?" Carol asked, not realizing that they were on the air.

"Because, although we won that money on 'Stunts & Stumpers,' it's still classed as income, and we'll have to pay the tax on it," Mike replied.

Danny Daniel was waving frantically.

"So?" Carol asked.

"It will boost us into a higher bracket," Mike said. "And the result will be that we'll have to pay a higher tax. It will be *so much* higher, in fact, that it will not only wipe out all our winnings but eat into our other income. In short, we'll be losing on the deal."

Danny Daniel was chewing frantically on his whip, while his assistant did the waving for him, trying to get Mike's and Carol's attention.

"That's terrible," Carol said. "We're being penalized for being so brilliant and winning all those prizes. Couldn't you sort of rearrange the figures somehow?"

"You mean cheat?" Mike asked.

"Of course not. But it isn't fair. It wouldn't be cheating if—"

A riding boot went sailing between them. They looked toward Danny Daniel. One of his boots was missing they noticed. He was shaking a fist at them and at the same time pointing toward the red light on the camera. Mike and Carol looked at each other. A momentary expression of realization and horror passed across their faces. Then, like troupers, they recovered.

"Yes, it *was* a stunning opening!" Carol bubbled. "The play itself, of course, was absolutely *mar*-velous. But it was the first-night audience that really highlighted the entire evening."

"I don't even remember being at any play—that's how *mar*-velous it was," Mike replied grouchily. "But, as for the first-night audience, I thought it was a weary cliché. Whoever directed it—" He suddenly interrupted himself. "What am I talking about?" he asked Carol.

Off-camera, Danny Daniel clapped a hand to his brow and toppled over backwards in a dead faint.

"The *opening!*" Carol hissed at Mike. "And the Duke and Duchess—*remember?*"

"Who opened the Duke and Duchess?" he asked. "And, now that you mention it, why would anybody bother to open them? They're both empty."

"Mike!" Carol squeaked.

"Somebody call me?" Alice was heard asking. Then she appeared at the table, and slapped a bundle of envelopes down in front of Mike and Carol. "I brought the mail," she announced, facing the camera. "It's the same old stuff—all those overdue bills all over again. You two must owe everybody in the country."

"Alice!" Carol squeaked.

Mike was unable to manage even that. He stared at Alice, as if struck dumb.

167

"When I went out to get the mail I found the truant officer at the door again," Alice went on, still speaking directly at the camera. "He wanted to know why you kept the kids out of school again all last week. I lied to him like you told me to. I told him they were all sick in bed with ingrown toenails. But don't you think it's about time you stopped keeping them home to do the washing and ironing and grocery shopping? And you better stop letting that six-year-old drive the car to the grocery store without a license, too."

"Alice!" Carol squeaked.

Mike finally came to life. He leaped up. "What are you doing!" he demanded. "We're on the air!"

"Oh, sorry, sir," Alice said, continuing to face the camera. "I forgot that you told me never to mention anything that *really* happens around here when you're doing the show."

Off-camera, Danny Daniel, having regained consciousness, was lifted to his feet.

"Hark!" Alice said, cupping her ear with a hand. "I hear the patter of tiny feet. It must be your two children—all six of them!" She waved vigorously. "Now, kids!"

Greg, Marcia, Peter, Jan, Bobby and Cindy came romping into camera range, then collected around the table.

Danny Daniel clapped a hand to his forehead and toppled over backwards in a dead faint once more.

"It'th uth, Mommy and Daddy," Cindy said brightly, seeming to be reciting. "We jutht came

168

from tarring and feathering that mean old truant offither and riding him out of town on a rail—like you told uth to do. Aren't we cute!"

"Cute!" Mike roared. "You're not even you!"

"Cindy!" Carol squeaked.

"Say, that's what I call a sharp retort, babe," Greg said to Carol. "You have quite a wit. About half-size, I'd say."

"Greg!" Mike squeaked.

"Aha! The other half was just heard from!" Greg said, winking at the camera.

Mike found his full voice again. "Young man, you can go straight to your room!" he commanded.

"Yo-ho-ho—if I went straight I wouldn't be a member of this family!" Greg retorted.

"Go to your room!" Mike shouted.

Greg began a screaming, stomping tantrum. "Not 'til you buy me a new car!" he wailed. "My old car is dusty!"

Mike turned helplessly to the camera. "This isn't true!" he said, his voice cracking. "None of it! Honest! It just isn't true!"

Alice put two fingers between her teeth and let go with a shrill, ear-splitting whistle.

"That's not true, either!" Mike said, facing the camera. "She's really a wonderful—"

In response to the whistle, Fluffy and Tiger came scrambling onto the set. First Fluffy, then Tiger, leaped onto the table. They began racing in a circle, yapping, spitting, yowrling, yelping, barking!

"Please—don't believe it!" Mike yelled at the camera.

But he was drowned out by Greg's wailing and Fluffy's and Tiger's yapping, yowrling and yelping.

"Fluffy!" Carol squeaked. "Tiger!" she squeaked.

Off-camera, Danny Daniel, rising once more, stared flabbergasted and shocked at the scene for almost a full minute. Then, steeling himself against fainting again, he bellowed an order. "I want bloops! Bloop them all out! Give me bloops! Let me hear twenty minutes of solid bloops! Bloops! Do you hear me? Blooooooooooo-ooooooops!"

The red light on the camera went dark.

"We're off the air!" Danny Daniel shrieked happily. Then he clapped a hand to his forehead and toppled over backwards in a dead faint.

"You!" Mike roared at Alice and the children. "Do you know what you just did? You just destroyed two brilliant careers! Up to your rooms! All of you!"

"Does that mean me, too?" Alice asked meekly.

"All of you!"

"That'th all right with me," Cindy said. "I've been wanting to use thothe phoneth anyway."

"Watch it!" Marcia said to her. "The show's over. You could get in trouble talking like that."

With Alice in the lead, the spoilers marched off.

Mike dropped back into his chair. He looked

at Carol, stunned and totally bewildered. "What happened?" he asked.

"I don't know," Carol squeaked.

Solomon I. Solaman came barging up to the table. "I should have listened to myself when I warned me about you two!" he said. "Solomon I. Solaman is never wrong. 'Personalities who glitter like that will be impossible to handle!' I told myself. This proves it. Not only are *you* impossible to handle, but your offspring and your hired help and your pets are impossible to handle. The whole house is virtually *infested* with temperament! Depending on the reaction I get from the network, you may or may not consider this my resignation as your manager! Good day!"

He barged out.

Staggering, holding a hand to his head, Danny Daniel approached the table. He halted about a yard away. Mike started to put out a hand to stop him from falling.

"No, no! Don't touch me!" Daniel begged. "I don't want to catch it! Just . . . just . . . just promise me one thing . . ." he pleaded. "If anybody ever . . . ever, ever, ever . . . asks you who directed you . . . please tell them you never even *heard* of me. I assure you that's what *I'm* going to tell everybody . . . that I never ever, ever, *ever* heard of you!" He stumbled off.

"Talk about temperament," Mike muttered.

The cameraman came up to the table. He was about Mike's age and had a face like a tomato, round, ruddy and ripe. "Don't pay no attention to them characters," he told them. "I been looking at shows like this through that peephole on the camera for about ten years now, and this was the best I ever seen. Most of them shows, they just set around and talk. But this one had action."

Mike nodded appreciatively.

"Thank you," Carol squeaked.

"I liked it where the cat and dog was going around and round," the cameraman chuckled. "Man, that was action!"

Mike and Carol looked slightly ill.

"Well, that's TV," the cameraman told them. "None of the good stuff lasts. That guy was right that said it's vast waistband. Talk, talk, talk, never any action. You know what's the matter with you two? You're ahead of your time."

Mike and Carol rose and left the table.

"Tell the kids they was great, too!" the cameraman called after them.

They did not look back. But they nodded.

"I wonder where we can go," Mike said despondently. "I don't want to see anyone we know."

"You could lock yourself in the den again."

"That's the script girl's office, I think," Mike replied. "After what happened, she's probably in there cleaning out her desk . . . my desk . . . our desk . . . somebody's desk . . ."

"We could go down to the basement," Carol said.

"That's a good idea," Mike nodded. "There's never much traffic down there. We can be alone and . . . and try to figure out what happened . . ."

"Mike . . ."

"What?"

"I just remembered . . . this house doesn't have a basement . . ."

Mike sighed sorrowfully. "The whole day's been like that . . ." he said.

11.

Unfortunate enough not to have a house with a basement, Mike and Carol retired to the recreation room. There, deep in gloom, they sat facing each other, staring vacantly, trying to understand what had happened and how it had happened. By noon, they were beginning to show signs of life again. Every once in a while, Mike would open his mouth as if to speak; then, after a second of thought, he would close it again. Carol would occasionally sigh.

In the early afternoon, Mike finally managed to speak. "We were rolling along so smoothly," he said, perplexity in his tone. "It just seemed as if nothing could stop us."

"Secretly," Carol said, "I was wondering what Danny Daniel would say about us in his autobiography when he was name-dropping. I just assumed we'd be in it. I mean, I was so positive that we'd be names."

"Secretly," Mike said, "I was already plotting the chapter titles for my *own* autobiography."

"It's Alice's fault," Carol said.

"Only partly. It was probably her idea. But the children went along with it. They're all old enough to know better. And I've always taught the boys to have minds of their own."

"That's what I keep telling the girls—have a mind of your own."

"So, we can't blame it on Alice entirely," Mike said. He smiled slightly. "I imagine she supplied most of the lines, though," he said. "And, you'll have to admit, they were better than that professional writer wrote. 'So long.' That's a crime. He gets *paid* for that kind of thing."

"Well . . . I thought it was sort of good," Carol said.

" 'So long?' "

"It has believability. It's the kind of thing that real people say when they leave."

Mike sank into silence and gloom again.

Carol's eyes stared into space. "I don't hear anything from upstairs," she said. "Not even Danny Daniel's phones ringing."

"They're probably feeling so guilty they can't even talk," Mike said. "I suppose they thought—" He shrugged. "I don't know . . . what *did* they think, do you suppose, when they did that?"

"Maybe they were auditioning. Maybe they wanted a show of their own," Carol guessed.

"Alice, maybe . . . but not the children. Do you think they were jealous? I find that hard to believe. I've always told the boys not to be jealous."

Carol nodded. "Me, too. Have a mind of your own and don't be jealous, I've always told the girls."

"There was *some*thing behind it," Mike said, still puzzled. "Someday, I suppose, we'll find out. It's probably something deep . . . psychological . . . mystical, even . . ."

There was the sound of the doorbell.

"There's somebody at the door," Carol said.

Mike looked at her interestedly. "You know . . . I think you could write," he said. "That line you just fed me had a lot of believability."

Carol smiled thinly.

The doorbell rang again.

"Isn't Alice going to get that?" Mike said crossly.

"You sent her to her room."

"Oh . . . yeah, that's right." He got up and walked toward the front of the house. When he reached the door and opened it, he found Solomon I. Solaman standing in the entranceway. "If you came back to tear up your contract with us, we don't have a contract," he said.

"You have a fantastic sense of humor," Solomon I. Solaman told him. "That's a great asset for a personality—just as long as he keeps it from the public." He moved past Mike, entering the house. "I underrated you," he said. "I didn't realize at first what you were doing. But it was marvelous. I can see that now. Where is our other little personality?"

"Alice, Greg, Marcia, Peter, Jan, Cindy, Bobby, Fluffy, Carol or the dog?"

"Carol, of course. I don't even know those other people."

Mike pointed toward the recreation room.

Solomon I. Solaman floated off in that direction, and Mike closed the door, then tagged after him. He found Solomon I. Solaman standing in the middle of the room gazing at Carol admiringly.

"I think something has happened," Mike said to Carol.

She winced. "Again? I didn't think there was anything left that *could* happen."

"Magnificent!" Solomon I. Solaman said.

Mike sat down and waited for the next blow to fall.

"If I were wearing a hat, I would take my hat off to you," Solomon I. Solaman said.

Mike and Carol sat up a little straighter.

"Until today," Solomon I. Solaman told them, "I have had nothing but contempt for personalities. Oh, I have always respected them for their ability to pretend to be something they were not, or, in short, their talent for fooling most of the people most of the time. But, down deep in my soul of souls, I have always felt that, if I had the time, I could do what they were doing better— or, in short, fool all of the people all of the time. Today, though, I saw genius at work. Two personalities proved to me that they are worthy of my honest respect." He bowed low. "I bow to you!"

Mike and Carol sat erect.

"I am a big enough man, too, to admit that I

didn't recognize genius at first," Solomon I. Solaman said, straightening. "The people . . . the little people . . . the unwashed masses . . . had to rise up and shout 'Hurrah! Hurrah!' before I got the message."

"Uh . . . the little people . . . are you talking about the children?" Mike asked.

"The children? Of course not."

"The cat? The dog?"

"The audience! The viewers!" Solaman replied. "Once more, they have proved the truth of the old adage!"

"Okay . . . what old adage?"

"The old adage: Solomon I. Solaman is always right!"

"That's a lot like that other old adage: Solomon I. Solaman is never wrong," Mike said. "But, how do you figure it? You said we'd be a hit."

"And that's what you are!" Solaman replied. "You're a hit! I just came from the television station. It's surrounded by an angry mob. All because of 'The Mike & Carol Show'!"

"They want to lynch us!" Carol said.

"No, no! They want to lynch the television station. Because you were cut off the air. The viewers love you! They adore you! And do you know why?"

"An epidemic of mental illness?" Mike guessed.

"Because they identify with you," Solomon I. Solaman told Mike and Carol. "You and your whole family. They look at you and they see themselves. What—now think about this: What

178

is the most pleasurable thing in the world for a human being?"

"It's to—" Carol began.

"Exactly," Solaman broke in. "To look in a mirror. And that's what the viewers were doing when they were watching you and your horrible family. They were looking at you and seeing themselves. They *loved* it!"

Mike and Carol looked at each other, then back at Solomon I. Solaman.

"There was a word in there . . ." Mike said. "It sounded a little like . . . uh, like 'horrible.' "

"Yes?" Solaman replied.

"We have a horrible family?" Carol asked. "We sort of thought—"

"Horrible only in a nice, typically human, money-making way," Solaman told her. "Don't you remember the show at all? It opened with you and Mike planning to cheat on your income tax. Typical—right? What could be more American?"

"Actually, I think it's more French," Mike said.

"Aha! Yes! But the viewers do not know that. Most of them think of it as being typically American. Just as they think that apple pie is American, when, actually, the apple pie was invented by a Chinese, who, after tasting it, rejected the whole concept."

"Really?" Carol said, interested. "Gee . . . why?"

"Unfortunately, he got a tough crust," Solaman replied. "And, thinking that all apple pies would be that way, he—please . . . you're distracting me. What is important is that your family came across as a mirror image of the families of the viewers. First, we had the mother and father, greedy, dishonest. Then the maid—winner, hands down, of the best supporting slob award. And the children were great, too. It was so obvious that they were the kids of the parents. Thoroughly obnoxious. Brats!"

"That's not the way they are," Carol protested weakly. "Really. They're wonderful children. They're kind and considerate and polite and—"

"Marvelous!" Solaman said. "We'll use that on the next show. The mother, describing her children, proving that she has absolutely no awareness of what they are truly like. Is that typical? Perfect! Oh, yes, you two are fabulous. The maid and the kids were fine—great support—but you two were really magnificent. Mike, your reaction to that one kid's temper tantrum was really beautiful. You screamed right back at him. It showed us exactly where he learned to put on a first-class tantrum. He got it from daddy. And, Carol, the way you sat around and squeaked throughout the whole terrible experience. Spectacular! It was the perfect picture of the typical mother reacting to a family crisis. Loved it!"

"That's *not* how we are!" Mike erupted.

"Take it easy," Solaman replied. "The camera is gone—hold the tantrum."

"But, we're not like that. Honestly," Mike insisted.

"Don't tell *me* what you're like," Solaman replied. "I have you on tape. There you are in black and white."

"But—" Mike began.

"But—" Carol said.

They exchanged defeated looks. Then, in unison, they sighed sadly.

"Remember earlier when I was asking 'what happened?'" Mike said. "I think I know the answer now."

Carol smiled softly. "Wasn't that sweet . . . Alice and the children were trying to save us from becoming what I guess we must look like on tape."

"We owe them an apology," Mike said.

"What's all this?" Solomon I. Solaman asked, concern in his voice. "This is not typical. What's this act you're putting on?"

Mike looked at him steadily for a second. "How do you know it's not typical?" he asked.

"In the first place, I heard myself say it. And Solomon I. Solaman is never wrong. In the second place, if what you did on the the show isn't typical, how could all those viewers identify with it?"

"Maybe because it's only typical of the viewers who expressed themselves," Mike replied. "How many were there in that mob that was storming the television station?"

"Thousands!"

"How many thousands?"

"All right, maybe there were only hundreds. But the television station was impressed."

"How many hundreds?" Carol asked.

181

"Who counted? Maybe not hundreds. But it was a fair-size crowd. At least ten . . . fifteen . . . twenty . . . well, maybe only five or six. But they were *very* noisy. The manager of the television station hid in his closet he was so impressed."

"He should have counted instead," Mike said. "And, even if he *had* counted a thousand, he should have asked himself if they represented everybody. Those other thousands—the one who didn't go to the studio—didn't they count for anything?"

"Are you trying to tell me something?" Solomon I. Solaman asked.

Mike nodded, smiling. "This hit quits," he replied.

Solaman looked as if he had received a surprise blow from behind. He peered at Mike for a second, astonished, then turned to Carol.

"I'm with him," she said, indicating Mike.

"But . . . but . . . to coin a phrase . . . the sky is the limit!"

"We reached our limit earlier this morning," Mike told him. "Now, we're back to earth. And that's where we intend to stay. 'The Mike & Carol Show' is finished. Unless you can find yourself another Mike & Carol."

Solaman brightened slightly. "You know . . . that's an idea. Danny Daniel has a family, I understand. And, from what I'm told, it's really typical." He moved toward the doorway. "If I can just get Danny and his wife to change their names . . ." He was floating at a faster rate.

"And we'll need six obnoxious kids . . . Perhaps we can adopt a few . . ."

He was gone.

Mike and Carol jumped up and threw their arms around each other and kissed.

"Free!" Carol said.

The doorbell rang.

"I'll bet that's him again," Mike said, going to answer it. "He probably wants Alice for the new 'Mike & Carol Show.' I don't think he believed me when I told him *none* of us are really like we were on television."

"Don't let him talk to her," Carol called after him. "The way Alice was looking into that camera, I think she has show business in her blood. She might be tempted to take him up on the offer."

Mike reached the door and opened it. "The answer—" he began.

But he found Jackie Jackson, not Solomon I. Solaman, outside. Jackson looked haggard and terrified. He bolted through the doorway.

"Close it!" Jackson said to Mike. "I think I lost them. Don't let them see that I came in here. They probably want to photograph it. Evidence. I can just see it at the trial. A big blowup of me at your front door!" He shuddered. "Who would believe that I just happened to be in the neighborhood?"

"Is that why you're here—because you just happened to be in the neighborhood?" Mike asked, puzzled.

"Are you kidding? Why would I be in this neighborhood? I don't know anybody here."

"You know us," Mike pointed out.

"I deny it!" Jackson snapped. "I never saw you before in my life!" He tried to get control of his emotions. "What am I saying? Of course I know you. That's why I'm in this mess. And they have tapes of 'Stunts & Stumpers'—they can prove I know you! We're sunk," he told Mike. "Sunk, I say! Do you understand? Sunk!"

Mike nodded. "I get the idea," he replied. "I don't really understand, though."

Jackson went to a window and looked out. "I don't see them," he reported. "That proves they're undercover men, doesn't it?"

"Who is it you don't see?"

"Buck Artwald's spies. He's having me followed."

"Are you sure? How do you know?"

"I sense it," Jackson replied. "I'm a very sensitive person. I sense things like that." He lowered his voice. "Where can we talk?"

Mike pointed toward the recreation room. "In there. That's where Carol is."

"Can we trust her? How well does she know Buck Artwald?"

"Not at all."

"Yeah, sure . . . that's what she tells *you*," Jackson said, moving on toward the recreation room. Then, entering, he called out to Carol, "Hi, there! Buck Artwald said to say 'Hello!' "

"I don't even know him," Carol replied.

"Okay, you passed the test," Jackson informed her.

Carol looked at Mike for an explanation.

"He thinks Artwald is having him followed," Mike explained. "Why, I'm not sure."

Jackson sank into a chair. "He has the goods on us, that's why," he said. "Remember what I told you? He got a bee in his bonnet that the show was fixed. Now he has the proof!"

"But you told us it wasn't fixed," Mike said, showing worry.

"It wasn't. It isn't. It never has been," Jackson replied. "But what good does that do? Artwald has proof!"

"How can he have— Maybe you better explain it."

"*Me* explain it?" Jackson said. "You two are the ones who're going to have to explain it." He looked at Mike and Carol disappointedly. "Why did you do it to me?" he asked. "I looked upon myself as your best friend."

"We only met you a few weeks ago," Mike replied. "And we only saw you at the TV studio."

"That's right—kick me when I'm down."

"What is it we've done to you—besides kicking you when you're down?" Carol asked.

"You rigged the show, that's what you did!"

Mike shook his head.

"Artwald can prove it!"

"But we didn't."

"What's *that* got to do with it? I keep telling you—*he can prove it!*"

185

"How?" Mike demanded.

"Your friend on the inside," Jackson replied. "The cousin of the lady from whom you got the tickets to the show who works in the steno pool!"

Mike and Carol looked at each other. Then they faced Jackson again.

"As I understand that, you're telling us that my friend Maggie, who gave us the tickets, works in your steno pool." She shook her head. "She doesn't."

"But her cousin does! And she got the tickets to the show from her cousin and then passed them on to you to throw us off the track," Jackson said. "Ver-ry clever!"

Carol shook her head again. "She just offered me the tickets and I just *accepted* them, that's all," she said. "There wasn't anything clever or underhanded or anything about it."

"Besides, what difference does it make where we got the tickets?" Mike asked.

"Collusion," Jackson replied. "That means getting together with somebody on the inside and pulling the wool over everybody's eyes. Your friend's cousin is an employee of the TV station. How do we know she didn't get hold of the questions before the show and slip them to you?"

"Don't you keep them locked up or something?" Carol asked.

"Of course. She couldn't possibly have got hold of them."

"Then what's the problem?" Mike asked.

"But who would believe that?" Jackson replied. "If you read in Buck Artwald's column that there was collusion going on, would you believe that your friend's cousin couldn't possibly get hold of those questions? Of course not. I wouldn't believe it myself." He slipped further down in the chair. "We're sunk!"

"What exactly is it that Artwald knows?" Mike asked. "That Maggie has a cousin who works for the TV station and that she gave the tickets to Maggie and Maggie gave the tickets to us? Is that all?"

"That's enough!"

Mike shook his head. "I doubt it. Not if we didn't gain anything from being on the TV show."

"But . . . all those prizes," Jackson said. "A year's supply of pipe cleaners is not nothing. And the sky-diving lessons, and—"

"We'll give it all back," Mike told him.

Jackie Jackson pushed himself up a bit in the chair. "What's your angle?" he asked suspiciously.

Mike smiled. "We just want to do something nice for you, our best friend," he answered.

"Cut it out—I hardly know you two birds."

"All right. The truth is that those prizes would cost us more in income tax payments than they're worth."

"Now, *that* is believable!" Jackson grinned, sitting up straight. He winked. "Just between us, though, what's the *real* truth?"

"Maggie is threatening to rat on us if we don't increase her cut of the loot," Carol told him.

Jackson nodded knowingly. "It figures."

"In return for doing this for you, you'll have to do something for us, however," Mike said.

"That figures, too," Jackson replied.

"You'll have to let us drop out of the show."

Jackson looked extremely pained. "But you're great," he said. "My rating is the highest it's ever been." He frowned. "That *would* get Artwald off my back, though," he said. "Okay—it's a deal. How will we explain it?"

"In the usual way," Mike replied. "Just tell your viewers that we quit 'for personal reasons.' "

"I know just how to say it—with a tear in the eye," Jackson replied. "That'll get 'em. I wonder if I could drag it out for a few weeks—just to keep the rating up."

Mike shook his head. "Make it a quick, clean break," he said. "It's always best that way."

"Sure, sure, I agree. But quick and clean for the first week and then a quick, clean rerun of the tape the second week." He saluted briskly. "Don't worry about it—I'll work it out." He got up and headed for the doorway. "It's like I always tell myself," he said, "if I really work at it, there's no problem too big for me to solve. Anytime in the future when you have problems, just give me a ring."

"Yes, we'll—" Mike began.

But Jackson was gone.

"Does that mean we're definitely retired from show biz?" Carol asked.

Mike put an arm around her, grinning. "Definitely. 'The Mike & Carol Show' made its debut and gave their farewell performance the same day."

Carol responded with mock applause. "Speech! Speech!"

"All right—bring me my audience."

For a second, Carol did not understand. Then she brightened and hurried from the room. A few minutes later, she returned. With her, looking repentant, were Alice, Marcia, Greg, Jan, Peter, Cindy and Bobby.

"Where are Fluffy and Tiger?" Mike asked.

"I couldn't interest them," Carol replied. "Anything you have to say to them, I think you'll have to put it in writing—on a piece of fish for Fluffy and a dog biscuit for Tiger." She indicated the others. "I brought the most dangerous prisoners, though."

Alice and the children had lined up, eyes averted. Mike stood in front of them. "Prisoners," he said, speaking severely, "as the official spokesman for 'The Mike & Carol Show,' I have assembled you here to inform you that—" His tone softened. "—that Mike and Carol would like to apologize."

There was a moment of silence. Then, as one, Alice and the children raised their eyes.

"—and ask you to forgive us," Carol added.

"We're all thtanding in the wrong plathes," Cindy said. "That'th what we were thuppothed to thay to you."

"All right, then," Mike smiled. "Let's make it a general, all-round, all inclusive apology and acceptance combined—agreed?"

189

There was a loud shout of approval.

"One thing more," Mike said. "The next time you catch Carol and me putting on a public spectacle and acting like the world's two prize boobs, you have permission to straighten us out, the same way you did this time. But . . . on second thought, check your plan with one of us first, will you?"

"Does this mean we don't have to stay in our room anymore?" Bobby asked.

The others all laughed.

"That's pretty much what it means," Mike replied.

"What now?" Marcia asked. "I'm so used to spending most of my time grumbling about the things that were going on around here that I got out of the habit of doing other things."

"I know what I'm going to do," Mike said. He looked at his watch. "It's still early afternoon. I'm going to take the rest of the day off and go to work. If I don't, I may discover I don't have an office to go to anymore." He headed for the doorway. "I'll see you all—"

The ringing of the phone interrupted him.

"Just a minute, dear," Carol said. "It might be for you."

Mike halted, waiting.

Carol picked up the recreation room extension. The call was from Maggie, who had given her the tickets to "Stunts & Stumpers." Carol signaled to Mike to continue waiting, thinking that the call might have some connection with the quiz

190

show. The conversation was brief, however. And the pleasant way in which Carol talked indicated that "Stunts & Stumpers" was not involved.

"All clear," Carol said to Mike, smiling, when she hung up. "It was about something entirely different. I guess Maggie isn't angry at me any more for being on that quiz show. She called me to—" The color suddenly drained from her face. "Oh, no! What did I do!"

Mike rushed to her. "Carol! What is it?"

"That call!" Carol said. "Maggie's church— it's raising funds. And they're raffling off a car. She asked me to buy some chances. She's sending one of the little girls who's selling the chances over to the house—right now—she's on the way —right now!"

Mike was baffled. "Well, fine," he said. "What's the matter with that?"

"The car that's being raffled off," Carol said "The company that makes the car is going to feature the winner on a TV commercial."

"Well . . . okay, so what?"

"Mike! How can you say that? You know what happened to us the last time we were on TV!"

Mike laughed. "Honey, we're not going to win that car. I have bought enough chances on cars in my life to . . . to . . . to stuff a car. I've *never* won."

"Mike, we'll win! Believe me! We'll win!" Carol said. "And we'll be in the commercial! And some talent manager will see that we're born personalities! And, Mike . . . Mike, we'll have to go through it all over again! The fans! The auto-graphs! Another Solomon I. Solaman! A new 'Mike & Carol Show'!"

Mike was shaking his head. "It couldn't happen twice."

"Mike, trust me, I know!" Carol said. "If we take a chance on that car, we'll win! Mike, let's not take a chance by taking a chance!"

"You say the girl is on her way over here?" Mike asked.

"Yes! We don't have a second to lose!"

"All right!" Mike said, facing Alice and the children. "This is it! Close and lock the windows. Pull the shades! Lock the doors! Post signs! Danger—Blasting! House for Sale! Anything to discourage visitors! Pile furniture in front of the doors! Let's go!"

The whole family stampeded from the recreation room to carry out the orders.

"Take the phone off the hook!" Mike bellowed. "And . . . somebody . . . talk to that dog and the cat. One bark . . . one meow . . . and they spend all day tomorrow in their rooms!"